second chances at the chocolate blessings cafe

STEENA MARIE HOLMES

second chances at the chocolate blessings cafe

A story based on chocolate and love
(You might think there's too much chocolate in this book, but I
disagree… lol)

A sweet inspirational romance novel
by Steena Holmes
Writing as Steena Marie Holmes

(Original pub date 2005)

who is steena marie?

This is the softer, sweeter side of NY Times and USA Today Bestselling Author Steena Holmes.

Writing as *Steena Marie Holmes,* you can expect stories filled with sweet treats, honest hearts and the craving to having something warm in your hand to drink.

Visit Steena Holmes
to find out more about the author and her books
ps...plus grab a free book or two on her website.

second chances at the chocolate blessings cafe

Forget love - just pass the chocolates! (and the coffee, blanket, tissues and a good book to read)

Alone. No groom. All eyes on her...it's a brides worst nightmare.

Left at the alter, everyone blaming her for the groom's cold feet, all Wynne can do is place a smile on her face and take one step forward: right into the arms of chocolate, because, chocolate is a jilted bride's best friend, after all.

With a not-so-secret passion for chocolate, Wynne focuses all her energy on making her new business venture - Chocolate Blessings, a store full of chocolate and gifts, a success. Which really isn't all that hard, think about it – what woman doesn't like chocolate?

But, despite all this, Wynne can't ignore those sweet and utterly delectable dreams of love that refuse to go away.

In her dreams, Wynne is dancing in the arms of a very strong and handsome man. But which man? Is it the one she turned away from years before out of fear, or the one who left her standing at the altar? Wynne has no sweet clue.

To the surprise of her best friends, Wynne finds herself knee-deep in planning her ex-fiancé's engagement party. In the whirlwind that occurs, Wynne must decide which man she is still in love with – the one who walked away or the one in her dreams.

This sweet romance is sure to touch your heart and have you looking for some chocolate to eat. This novel is a Christian / Inspirational Romance.

would you like a free read?

I have two books for you to choose from if you'd like to sign up for my newsletter. I send out one email a month, sharing updates, book sales, what I'm reading and even a delicious recipe I've tried that month.

Choose between Halfway to Nowhere or Stillwater Shores... just click here to join my mailing list!

a note from steena marie

Hello!

First off, thank you so much for wanting to reading Wynne's story. Out of all my characters, she's the one that holds a special place in my heart - maybe because she was the first chocoholic I ever wrote about, or maybe it's because there is so much of me in her. Either way...Wynne is very special to me and I hope she'll become special to you as well.

I hope you'll enjoy the story. This was my first novel I'd ever written - way back in 2005. At the time, it won a publishing contract thanks to a contest I'd entered...and thus began my journey in writing. Now, I need you to remember something...this was the VERY first book I'd ever written. I never took a writing class, had no idea about tenses and plots or anything else...

With that in mind...as I went through this book, I had to stop myself from rewriting it...it's rough, obviously written by a 'new writer' but the heart is there and I hope you enjoy it.

Before you turn the page, I will warn you...you may feel a sudden craving for chocolate while reading. It seems like my characters are always eating chocolate, cake and drinking coffee or hot cocoa...if only we could live our lives like that...

Enjoy!

Steena

PS...thanks to the advice of my reader group, I've added recipes for desserts mentioned in this book. You'll find them sprinkled throughout the book, in between chapters (as they recommended).

PSS...there's a special reader note at the end of this book, just for you!

CHAPTER ONE

love is overrated

C hocolate was a jilted bride's best friend.

I would know.

For the happy bride on her wedding day, it was the little things that made her smile; the lingerie wrapped with vanilla-scented beads, the gorgeous white satin wedding gown on the padded hanger, the friends and family who filled the pews, the ring on her finger, the photographer snapping memories for years to come.

But for the jilted bride…it's none of those things.

It for sure was not the groom who ran away, nor the meaningful cards full of well wishes and deepest sympathies that accompanied the overwhelming-but-definitely-appreciated boxes of chocolates that arrived on my doorstep.

No - I take that back. Those people made me smile. I loved those people.

It was the groom who high-tailed it out the rectory windows in his black tuxedo and chocolate-colored satin cummerbund, that I preferred to forget.

It was a beautiful color, by the way. Imagine the color of milk chocolate as it melts on your fingertip, you know – that delectable aroma that tantalized you until the only thing you could do was lick that tiny smear off your finger? THAT color.

My bridesmaids looked beautiful, and the cake – was absolutely stunning. A three-tiered, white iced, triple-brownie cake wrapped in a simple chocolate-colored ribbon.

Elegant, simple, and satisfyingly me, to a T.

Elegant. Simple. Satisfying. Stunning. Sad. So very, very sad.

Love was overrated, and I was done with it.

But, as I laid on my uber-soft couch bawling my eyes out while I watched, for the umpteenth time, the unforgettable scene between Sandra Bullock and Keanu Reeves in the Lake House, I knew I would take it all back if I could.

I would have given anything and everything to be loved. Again. Like I was before my fiancé realized I wasn't enough for him.

As Keanu took Sandra in his arms and drew her close for their unforgettable kiss, I reached over to grab another Kleenex off the coffee table, but misread the distance and ended up reaching way too far just as my front door opened.

"Hello, darlin'." A friendly voice called out.

"Ugh, in here, Heather." I wasn't sure if she heard me or not, seeing how my lips were kissing the carpet.

Tilting my head for air, I noticed a pair of red-heeled shoes, sitting beside a brown canvas bag bulging at weird angles. I looked up to find Heather covering the telltale signs of a smirk showing through her splayed fingers.

"What are you doing?" she said. "I thought you were sick, and here you are, doing gymnastics…I think? Although," she mused, "that position does look kind of interesting." Heather squatted on the floor with her head tilted to get a better view of my face.

"Oh, just help me up, will you?"

With a little bit of grunting and stretching of body parts I didn't know I had, we managed to push my body back on the couch. I squished back down into my warm place and sighed.

My uber-soft couch enveloped me like my mother's hand-stitched blanket. I was in warmth heaven. When I caught Heather's gaze, I tried to make the most pathetic-looking face I could manage, hoping for sympathy.

"Yeah, nice try. By the way - gymnastics are not your forte." Heather lifted up her overflowing bag. "I brought over some treats for you," she said over her shoulder as she made her way into my kitchen.

"Have I told you I love you?" I asked her. I don't even bother to ask how she knew I was home today.

My pampering angel was Heather Manning, a gourmet chef who just happened to be one of my closest friends and ex-roommate.

"You forget I'm married to your business partner. He called to tell me how pathetic you sounded this morning. I'm here to rescue you, and to keep you from contaminating the store. Call me your personal pampering guardian." Heather curtsied. Tall, elegant, and without an inch of fat on her body, her curtsy would do any princess proud.

"I'm also here with strict instructions to make sure you don't go to work today," she said as she brought me a steaming cup of tea. Hmmm, hot honey and lemon.

"But don't touch me, cough on me, or expect me to pick up all your nasty Kleenex," she said, glancing around the room, disdain evident by her puckered brow. "Drink your tea."

"Please tell me you brought me your famous chicken noodle soup," I begged.

Her soup is literally on par with her chocolate, my chocolate, or anyone else's chocolate. It was that good.

"What kind of friend would I be if I left you here in misery without my soup?" Heather said. "Now, just relax. Dream of something sweet, or maybe some handsome fellow bringing you chocolate. I'll wake you when the soup is heated."

I liked the idea of having my dream man bring me chocolate. Being the good girl that I am, I try to always do as I'm told, so dream away I would.

"You're a sweetie," I mumbled as I burrowed underneath my blanket. "Even if you did leave me to get married, I still think you're the best."

As I drifted off to sleep, I heard her laughter in the background.

heather's healing chicken noodle soup

There's nothing like a bowl of chicken noodle soup when you are feeling under the weather. Turn the page for Heather's Healing Chicken Noodle Soup recipe! (Ps...this is the only type of soup I'm able to make that actually tastes good).

HEATHER'S HEALING CHICKEN NOODLE SOUP RECIPE

INGREDIENTS:

- 1 tbsp olive oil
- 2 stalks celery (diced)
- 2 med carrots (diced)
- 1 yellow onion (diced)
- Salt and pepper
- 4 cups of broth & 4 cups of water
- Chicken breasts (as much/little as you want)
- Pasta - any type of noodle you want

STEPS:

- In a large pot, cook celery, carrots, onion until carrots are crisp and tender (about 5 min). Season with salt and pepper.
- Add broth and water and bring to a boil.
- Add chicken and simmer. Cover and cook until chicken is done (about 10 min).
- Remove chicken and chop or shred as desired.
- Add pasta and cook until tender (4 min)
- Season with salt and pepper to taste

Add dill if you like to the top.

Serve in a nice size bowl. Add crackers or toast.

If you make this when you are sick…feel better soon.

If you're making this because who doesn't like soup on a cold day…I hope you enjoy!

CHAPTER TWO

the dream

T he three days I'd spent at home were glorious.
Glorious and oh-so boring. I'd done nothing but watch rom-coms and sleep.

I had the most amazing dreams. Some people dreamed of random things, like driving in cars or flying through space. Me, I dreamed of romance, of love, and always in the most amazing places, too.

Take the one I just woke up from, for instance:

I was in a ballroom decorated to perfection. There was an orchestra in the far corner. Soft music could be heard drifting throughout the room. The whole room was lit by candlelight. Waiters in black tuxedos walked through the throngs of people, offering glasses of sparkling champagne.

I was dancing in the arms of a very strong, handsome man. The man haunts my dreams nightly, leaving my heart aching every morning for the promise of what could have been. Tonight, he wore a black tux with a hint of cologne that I knew would always be just beyond my reach.

He was the man of my dreams.

I never looked into his face, yet I knew him deep in my heart.

We were dancing. I was wearing a gorgeous Vera Wang gown

that swept behind me as we moved across the floor. In graceful steps, ones resembling Ginger Rogers and Fred Astaire, we swayed to the beautiful music.

I felt secure, wanted, and loved. It was the perfect night. I turned my head to gaze into his eyes. Tonight was the night. The night that I'd finally tell him how I feel. The night I'd finally look into his face. As my eyes slowly rose I...THUMP.

I was on the floor.

It was amazing how much pain one experiences as one fell from their bed. Not only did my head hurt from hitting my nightstand, but my shoulder twisted under me in a way that was uncomfortable, my flannel nightgown was wrapped around my legs so tightly that I couldn't move them if I tried, and I think I landed on my nose.

With my free hand, I gingerly touched it and realized I was bleeding.

Just great. My first nosebleed ever, and it was from falling out of bed.

By some miraculous feat, I untwisted myself as the phone rang. With a disgruntled tone that is somewhat muffled by the Kleenex stuck up my nose, I answered and said something that resembled 'hello'.

"Well, good morning to you too, sunshine. Don't tell me I just woke you up. It's already eight am. You're not sounding that great, maybe you should get right back into bed and stay home again. Matt and Lily can handle the store for another day," Heather said in her bubbly voice.

"My nothe ith bleeding. Call you bach," I said as I ran into the bathroom. I was surprised my mirror didn't crack from my reflection. My head was tilted up to stop the bleeding, my hair was in wild disarray, and I had drool lines trailing down the pillow's marks leading to the one side of my mouth.

Quite attractive if I said so myself.

I still couldn't believe I'd fallen out of bed. The memory of my dream lingered, and I could feel strong arms around me as we were dancing to soft music. If only reality could be like my dreams, I would be happy and satisfied.

With my head tilted so I could count the dust bunnies hanging from my bedroom ceiling, I called Heather back.

"Was there an honest-to-goodness reason for calling me so early in the morning?"

"Umm, I think you want Heather," Matt answered. "Listen, if you're still sick, stay home." I heard the phone drop and his voice in the background, "I don't know what you did, but Wynne doesn't sound too happy. Good luck."

"Wynne? Did you fix your nose? What happened?" Heather said. Her voice was too chipper. Way too chipper.

"Apparently, beds aren't meant for dancing, and I fell out during a pirouette. I hit my nose on the floor. No, don't laugh. It was a perfectly good dream, too. I almost saw his face this time."

Heather knew all about my dreams. I'd been having them for the past year or so. At first, I found it very exciting, dreaming about a man deep in my heart I knew that I knew. At least, I think I knew him. I've yet to see his face. Now it's getting downright frustrating.

If this was God's way of preparing me for a new love life, He has a funny way of doing it.

"You almost saw his face? Wow. Go back to bed then and start dreaming again. I still say that it's Rich you're dreaming of," Heather said.

"It can't be Richard. We've already gone through this. He's got to be married by now. Along with the two kids, a dog with a loving wife to hand him coffee every morning. I can't be dreaming of him. That would just be wrong." I said. "He's been out of my life far too long for me to start thinking of him again. Nope, this has to be someone else. Someone who can take his place in my heart." Maybe I'm in denial.

"You don't know he's married, Wynne. You just think he is," Heather said. "You heard he was getting married, but maybe, and this could be true, he didn't actually get married. Did you ever think he could be like you?"

I closed my eyes. She was going to say it. I knew she would.

"You guys are soul mates. You need to find him."

"And what do I do when I do find him? Do I call him up? What if his wife answers or his girlfriend? How do I explain to them or to him the reason for my call? No. I don't think so."

"All right, live in your dream world," Heather said. "The reason I called was to tell you I'm sending a surprise over with Matt this morning. This is the official phone call to tell you to keep your hands off. I want you to have complete deniability, at least for the first customer. You'll need to add your own little personal touch to the boxes, but do not look inside. Got it?" Heather hung up.

That was so not fair. Knowing her, she'd made up something that tasted delicious. She always did that to me. She made me wait, along with everyone else, to find out what it was. I used to peek, but I've experienced her wrath too often to do that anymore.

She doesn't play fair. And she knew it, too.

In anticipation of what I will find when I get to the store, I quickly finished getting ready. I always find myself excited to go into my store. A new day waits, and it had been a few days since I was last there. I trusted Matt to keep it running smoothly, but he didn't quite have that woman's touch.

My phone rang as I headed out the door. My arms were full of lemon-raspberry streusel muffins I'd made last night, so I just let the answering machine take it. If it was important enough, they'd call my cell.

CHAPTER THREE

chocolate blessings

Chocolate Blessings, my grand passion.

At the jingle of my doorbells, I took a deep breath and sighed. The smell of chocolate and flowers was amazing. I co-owned my oasis with Matthew Manning, Heather's husband. With my love for chocolate and his business savvy, we made a great team, if I do say so myself.

The doors to the Chocolate Blessings Cafe had only been open for two years, but we already experienced more growth than I ever dreamed of.

With that growth came long hours, especially during the holiday season...like now, Christmas. One guess for what the number one gift everyone prefers to buy? You got it.

Who in their right mind would turn down chocolate?

Besides chocolate, we also helped our local community by taking in one-of-a-kind gift items made locally. Our hand-selected gift baskets were hot sellers right now.

Who knew that I could turn my love for chocolate into a profitable career?

Christmas music wafted throughout the store. Fresh flowers from our next-door florist bloomed on shelves, desks, and tables.

We offered a fresh cut rose free with every order – a little touch I found the female customers loved.

Our showcase of chocolate was fully stocked, shelves lined with gourmet boxes of chocolate, and I even set a few new gift ideas out.

Mental note to self: check out new gift ideas and find more.

Lily, our front clerk, greeted me warmly. "Wynne, thank-you-Jesus, you are back. It's been a long three days without you here. How are you feeling? You definitely look better. Oh, I have so much to tell you."

Lily, if you couldn't already tell, was a bouncy twenty-something. She'd be classified as the bubbly greeter in her young adults' group at church. Her bright smile and inviting laughter were always present.

She was the perfect person to have at the front counter.

"I missed your smiley face. Please tell me we have hot cider ready." I passed the container of muffins I brought in to her over the counter.

I decided to section off a small corner with some garden tables and chairs a few months ago. I thought it would be a wonderful place to sit and chat while enjoying a treat. We offered gourmet hot chocolate, flavored coffee and tea, and with the season upon us, warm apple cider.

The idea was a hit right away, and it was very rare that you didn't find the tables full of laughter. If you listened closely, you could hear satisfied sighs of delight once they breathed in their hot drink's aroma and tasted their chocolate treat.

"I just put on a fresh pot. That's been a hot commodity the past few days. Oh, and there was a message from Pastor Joy. If you were feeling up to it, they would still like to meet this morning here for coffee. I told her you would call her right away." Lilly said.

Every Thursday morning, a group of ladies from our local church met here for coffee. Their official group name was the

Latte Ladies. There are five of us who met for coffee, chocolate, and prayer.

These ladies were my morning cup of sanity many times over. Being the youngest of the bunch, I was often mothered and mentored by four older women on a regular basis.

I had to admit; I loved it.

Sure, I was a strong independent woman, but deep inside, I loved to be taken care of. It was my Latte Ladies who gave me the push to create Chocolate Blessings.

The bells above the door jingled as I poured myself a cup of hot cider. In walked Matthew, carrying brightly wrapped boxes.

"Well, good morning, Sunshine," he greeted me, using his nickname for me. "Good to see my wife's pampering did the job. Heather said you could put the ribbon thingies on these boxes." Matthew had a brilliant mind, one that was constantly running. The only thing was, along with that brilliant mind, he was also very logical and practical. While he agrees that the little things in our store helped to sell our product, trying to figure out just what little things we needed was beyond his comprehension.

"Ribbon thingies? You mean bows?" I grabbed a few of the boxes while trying to juggle my dripping cup of cider. Despite specific instructions not to peek, I was sorely tempted to go against Heather's orders. The delicious aroma escaping one of the boxes I was holding was almost too hard to resist.

I was hoping that Heather didn't tell him I wasn't allowed to peek. I disliked surprises with a passion, especially if I knew about them.

Especially when it comes to chocolate.

Keeping chocolate a secret was just not fair.

"I was there when Heather told you not to look. You're allowed to help wrap them all pretty like, but then that's it. These are the surprise thingies we decided to do," Matt said while trying to maneuver around all the displays, the front counter, and then around the office door in the back.

As we walked into our tiny office, the phone rang. Answering it, I heard, "put on fresh coffee 'cause we're coming over," giggles, and then click. I chuckled. The Latte Ladies.

That was Joan. She was quite the character. Always had a smile on her face, and you just can't help but smile when you saw her. I imagined that today she would wear some type of Christmas earrings that dangled, lit up, or sang a song along with her sparkling Christmas jacket.

"Who was that?" asked Matt. Then he looked at the calendar, saw the big coffee mug stickers that were placed on every Thursday, and groaned.

"Hey, get them to buy a box, and then you can see what is in them." What a nice guy, offering me a way out of having to willfully disobey one of Heather's many orders.

"I think I might just do that ... if you hurry and hand me the ribbons and bows."

After an hour or so fiddling with ribbons, I heard the doorbells jingling and laughter filling the store. My Latte Ladies had arrived.

"Hmmm, something smells good."

"Oh, she put apple cider on. She must love us."

"Chocolate and coffee – the best of friends."

"Oh, what do you have in those boxes? I want one."

As I juggled the boxes in my hand, the women came over to help me arrange them on the shelves. My mouth watered, knowing soon I would find out what is in the boxes.

"Oh, what do we have here? Hmmm, it smells delicious. Oh, and it's a secret. Wynne, where do you come up with the ideas? I'm gonna have to grab one of these. Tracey, you take one too--you need to put some weight on that body of yours. Judy, won't these be perfect gifts for our Secret Sisters' group? Oh, and we must add a few of these to the Christmas baskets. Pastor Joy, you know you can't turn down chocolate. Wynne, why do you always seem to be placing new products out when we arrive? Shame on you, like we could ever deny ourselves the pleasure of your sweets," Joan Hollingway fired off before taking a breath.

Meet Joan, the one lady in our group with the habit of talking rather quickly when she got excited. And if you hadn't already figured it out, chocolate in any form was her thing.

Probably why we bonded in the first place.

As each woman grabbed her box and cup of coffee or cider, we headed over to the café section of the store. I've made sure that I created this space with coziness in mind. It had the look of an outdoor café, but with the warmth of a country cottage. Cushions on each seat, hand-made tablecloths, and antique furniture grace the little corner. Many of my handmade items for sale were displayed in this area. From plaques, to stitchery designs, tattered pillows, and quilts. Handmade dolls, candles, sheep of all sorts, quilts, and fabric.

So many wonderful ladies created these products, and it's continually being updated with new products on a weekly basis. I firmly believed in showcasing their items, as a way of supporting them, just like how they were always there as a support to me.

Normally the first few minutes of each Thursday morning were spent pursuing all the new finds within that nook. After that, we'd gather at the table, get comfy, and delve right into each other's lives.

For the longest time, my life was a hot topic. Thankfully, no longer.

This time it appeared to be Tracey's turn. As much as she was one of my closest friends, I took delight in having the focus set on her for a change.

"So Tracey, how are the kids doing? Was Pastor Mike able to take a break from the church office and watch the little ones for you, or did you have to find a sitter?" Judy asked.

Tracey is married to Pastor Mike Wells, the youth pastor in our church. They had three children, and I used to envy her, until I took a few days off and helped around her home after the birth of her youngest. Now I just loaded her with chocolate every time I saw her. Whoever said raising children was easy must have had a full-time nanny.

"Little Miles is starting to get the hang of crawling, which means Josiah has to clean up his toys more. Katy is having a bit of a hard time with school. Mike and I have talked about home school, but I honestly don't think it's something I could handle right now," she admitted with a sheepish grin.

"Home school, Tracey. Are you out of your mind?" I said.

The glare Tracey sent my way made me bite my lip. "I said we were talking about it, not actually doing it. Mike has talked to a couple of our church families who homeschool, and they all claim that their children excel more at home. I just don't know," she sighed.

I felt a kick on my shin, and while I was rubbing it, I caught the dirty look given by Pastor Joy. I was the one who should be handing out the dirty looks; it's my shin that now hurt.

"Tracey, would you mind if we brought this to the Lord in prayer? This is obviously something that weighs pretty heavily on your heart, and it's the last thing you need to be worrying about right now?" asked Pastor Joy. She was great at hearing what people had to say and then directing those issues to God.

As Tracey nodded her head in agreement, Joan fiddled in her seat. She kept twisting the surprise box in her hands. "Oh, come on ladies, and let's hurry and open our boxes so we can see what goodies lie inside. I'm sure the good Lord will understand the need to have a bit of heaven in our mouths before we begin."

Finally. "Please do. Heather made me promise not to peek inside the boxes, so I can't wait to see what you have," I said.

"Well, we wouldn't want Wynne to break her promise, now would we?" A wide grin filled Judy's face. As they all slowly opened their surprise boxes, I leaned in, trying to peek.

Heather had created a masterpiece. A chocolate basket was inside each box with tiny little chocolate forms inside each basket.

Judy had a white chocolate basket filled with little chocolate apples. Pastor Joy had a milk chocolate basket filled with little Christmas tree-shaped chocolates. Tracey had the same basket but with baby sheep forms, and Joan had a dark chocolate basket filled with chocolate hearts.

Heather had truly outdone herself.

As each woman at the table savored her tiny piece of chocolate heaven, Pastor Joy brought out her Bible. We'd been dealing with how we view ourselves as daughters of God. It's been an interesting study, to say the least. It was one thing to actually say you are a child of God. It's another thing to believe it. It was all about how we viewed ourselves, which then, in turn, reflected on how we think God viewed us.

He loved us with unconditional love, but we're the ones who felt there should be limits and boundaries to His love for us. Silly, really. Why did we make simple things so complicated?

My favorite passage was in Psalms – "I will not die but live and proclaim what the Lord has done." No matter what happened in my life, I would give God the glory.

It was that same verse that helped me to hold my head high after the whole wedding fiasco.

After our prayer at the end, I gathered up all the coffee cups and empty chocolate boxes. I heard the jingle of the doorbells ring, and briefly glanced over to see who had walked in.

To my surprise, it was Nancy Montgomery. The bane of my very existence.

It's very rare that Nancy came into Chocolate Blessings.

To think once upon a time she was going to be my mother-in-law and now she blamed me for running her son out of town.

CHAPTER FOUR

sweet surprises

After an hour or so of fiddling with ribbons, I heard the doorbells jingling and laughter filling the store. My Latte Ladies had arrived.

"Hmmm, something smells good."

"Oh, she put apple cider on. She must love us."

"Chocolate and coffee – the best of friends."

"Oh, what do you have in those boxes? I want one."

As I juggled the boxes in my hand, the women came over to help me arrange them on the shelves. My mouth watered, knowing soon I would find out what was inside.

"Oh, what do we have here? Wynne, where do you come up with the ideas? I'm gonna have to grab one of these. Tracey, you take one, too--you need to put some weight on that body of yours. Judy, won't these be perfect gifts for our Secret Sisters group? Oh, and we must add a few of these to the Christmas baskets. Pastor Joy, you know you can't turn down chocolate." She turns to me, finger waggling as if I was being naughty.

"Wynne," she continues, "why do you always seem to be placing new products out when we arrive in the store? Shame on you, like we could ever deny ourselves the pleasure of your sweets," Joan Hollingway fired off before taking a breath.

Meet Joan, the one lady in our group who has a habit of talking rather quickly when she gets excited. And if you haven't already figured it out, chocolate in any form gets her excited.

As each woman grabbed her box and coffee, we headed over to the café section of the store. I've made sure that I created this space with coziness in mind. It has the look of an outdoor café, but with the warmth of a country cottage.

Cushions on each seat, hand-made tablecloths, and antique furniture grace this little corner. Since this is an area where you sit and chat, many of the handmade items for sale are displayed in this area. From candles and earrings to mugs and bagged tea, farmhouse decor, and sheep of all sorts, not to mention the hygge section that is quite popular.

So many wonderful ladies within the community create these products, and it's continually being updated on a weekly basis. I firmly believe in showcasing these items. I know personally how much love and care goes into every single stitch and design.

When Matt and I first opened Chocolate Blessings, we began with consignment items, until I realized many of the ladies who sell here consider this to be their one source of income for themselves.

Normally the first few minutes of each Thursday morning are spent pursuing all the new finds within this nook. After that, we gather at the table, get comfy, and delve right into each other's lives. For the longest time, my life was a hot topic. Thankfully, no longer.

This time it appeared to be Tracey's turn. As much as she is one of my closest friends, I took delight in having the focus set on her for a change.

"So Tracey, how are the kids doing? Was Pastor Mike able to take a break from the church office and watch the little ones for you, or did you have to find a sitter?" Judy asked.

Tracey is married to Pastor Mike Wells, the youth pastor in our church. They have been with us for the past four years now, and are loved by many. Tracey has three children, and I used to envy her, until I took a few days off and helped around her home after the birth of her youngest. Now I just load her with chocolate every time I see her.

Whoever said raising children was easy must have had a full-time nanny.

"Little Miles is starting to get the hang of crawling, which means Josiah has to clean up his toys more. Katy is having a bit of a hard time with school. Mike and I have talked about home school, but I honestly don't think it's something I could handle right now," she admitted with a sheepish grin.

"Home school, Tracey. Are you out of your mind?" I said.

The glare Tracey sent my way made me bite my lip. "I said we were talking about it, not actually doing it. Mike has talked to a couple of our church families who homeschool, and they all claim that their children excel more at home. I just don't know," she sighed.

I felt a kick on my shin, and while I was rubbing it, I saw Pastor Joy give me a dirty look. I was the one who should be handing out the dirty looks; it's my shin that now hurt.

"Tracey, would you mind if we brought this to the Lord in prayer? This is obviously something that weighs pretty heavily on your heart, and it's the last thing you need to be worrying about right now?" asked Pastor Joy. She's great at hearing what people have to say and directing things to God.

As Tracey nodded her head in agreement, I noticed Joan fiddling in her seat. She kept twisting the surprise box in her hands. "Oh, come on ladies, and let's hurry and open our boxes so we can see what goodies lie inside. I'm sure the good Lord will understand the need to have a bit of heaven in our mouths before we begin."

Finally. "Please do. Heather made me promise not to peek inside the boxes, so I can't wait to see what you have," I said.

"Well, we wouldn't want Wynne to break her promise, now would we?" Judy said, a wide grin filling her face. As they all slowly opened their surprise boxes, I leaned in.

Inside the boxes, Heather had created a masterpiece. There was a chocolate basket inside each box with tiny little chocolate forms inside each basket. Judy had a white chocolate basket filled with little chocolate apples. Pastor Joy had a milk chocolate basket filled with little Christmas tree-shaped chocolates. Tracey had the same basket but with baby sheep forms, and Joan had a dark chocolate basket filled with chocolate hearts. Heather had truly outdone herself.

As each woman at the table savored her tiny piece of chocolate heaven, Pastor Joy brought out her Bible. We have been dealing with how we view ourselves as daughters of God. It's been an interesting study, to say the least.

It's one thing to actually say you are a child of God. It's another thing to believe it. It's all about how we view ourselves, which then in turn, reflects on how we think God views us. He loves us with unconditional love, but we're the ones who feel there should be limits and boundaries to His love for us.

My favorite passage is in Psalms – "I will not die but live and proclaim what the Lord has done." No matter what happens in my life, I will give God the glory. It was this scripture that helped me to hold my head high after the whole wedding fiasco.

After our prayer at the end, where we prayed for Tracey, I gathered up all the coffee cups and empty chocolate boxes. I heard the jingle of the doorbells ring and briefly glanced over to see who had walked in.

To my surprise, it was Nancy Montgomery. The bane of my very existence. It's very rare that Nancy comes into Chocolate Blessings.

She blames me for running her son out of town.

I pretended not to see her. Maybe that way, she would not notice me and then hopefully leave. Past encounters have either left me in tears or made me want to scream. I don't know how she does it, but she leaves me quaking in my very shoes.

And to think, once upon a time, she was going to be my mother-in-law.

CHAPTER FIVE

the ice queen

"Mrs. Montgomery. So nice to see you. You came at just the right time. We have a new display called our Sweet Surprise. Don't you think the little boxes with bows are adorable? And just wait till you see what is inside – you won't be able to resist."

Thank goodness for Lily. As she chattered with Nancy, I tried to casually slink away.

Unfortunately, neither the slinking nor the chattering worked as a victorious diversion.

"Yes, Lily, I will take one of those boxes, but first I must speak with Wynne. I know she had her little Bible study this morning, so she must be here," Nancy said as she glanced around the store.

I knew she would spot me any moment. I stood up straight, grasped Judy's hand for a quick moment of strength, and called out a greeting which I hope didn't show my hesitation.

"Good morning, Nancy. You'll love what you find in those mystery boxes. Is there anything I can help you with?" I asked as I silently congratulated myself for not allowing my voice to quiver.

"Yes, actually, there is. Lily, be a dear and ring up a few of those boxes, as well as one of those little gift cards that you have, and have it say Welcome Home," she demanded as she walked towards me.

"Wynne, Jude is coming home today. His father is ill, and he is coming home to help with the business. Please leave him alone. My son has finally decided to return home to where he belongs. You broke his heart once; he doesn't need you to do it again." The cold gleam in her eye was enough to freeze hell over and beyond.

My heart dropped to the floor. It skipped a beat before slowly rising.

Ever since that fateful day when I wouldn't walk down the aisle, Nancy blamed me for her son skipping town three years ago and never coming back.

Never mind the fact that it was his decision to move away. She adamantly declared that I broke her son's heart.

While I did agree with her, doesn't she see that it hurt me too? I understood she was hurt and feels abandoned by her only child, but why did she continually take it out on me?

Nancy habitually gave me the cold shoulder whenever we met in church. She rarely came into my store, yet she always seems to know what was happening in my life.

Once upon a time, Nancy and I were very close. Jude was a major part of my life, and it just became natural to have a relationship with his mother. It was one thing to lose her presence in my life, but it was quite another thing to be treated as a stranger.

The joy of the Lord is to be my strength, but in that instance, I didn't feel very strong.

For three years, I pretended that the break up between Jude and me was mutual and that there were no hard feelings. When he decided to leave town, my heart broke. Not too many people knew what really happened between us. We both agreed it was better that way.

"Nancy, I am sorry to hear about your husband. You must be happy that Jude is coming home." I gave her a brief smile. "But the only relationship between Jude and me is friendship. I haven't seen him since he left, and although we've remained in touch here and there, what we had is all in the past. We've been over for a long time."

Did I really believe that? Deep in my heart, I knew we weren't meant for each other, but I still had feelings for him. Goodness – I almost married the guy, of course, I was still going to have feelings for him

"That is good to hear. Just make sure you keep it that way," Nancy said, as cold as the Ice Queen herself. Walking towards the front door, she stopped, turned her head, and dropped her final piece of news. "Jude has moved on with his life. He's even bringing a special friend with him for us to meet. He doesn't need you in his life to complicate things." The door slammed, leaving me with no response.

My body crumbled, my lungs shrunk in size, and I struggled for air. Thank goodness I hadn't moved away from the tables. I grasped onto the edge of the table, leaning on it while I sank to the floor.

Tracy placed her hand on my shoulder; Judy took hold of my hands and gave them a squeeze. Joan said the one thing she knew I needed to hear.

"I think this is the perfect time for some more chocolate."

Pastor Joy came over and gave me a brief hug. She leaned down and whispered in my ear, "I need to leave for the office, but Wynne, please give me a call if you need me. You are a strong woman of God who can get through this. I know you." She turned to whisper something to Judy before she walked away.

Lily came over with some chocolate in her hands. I absently took what she offered, briefly realizing that this was the chocolate I kept hidden away for emergencies. A friend sent me good chocolate from Belgium, and it only came out in dire need.

How did she know about my secret stash? I dismissed the thought as I savored the sweet decadence melting in my mouth. I was just glad she knew about it.

With a quick, "Lord, give me strength" prayer being uttered, I stood and tried to act as if nothing was wrong. It's a façade, a mask I often wore, but never really worked with this group of ladies. I gave them all a quick smile.

"I'm okay. It's been a long three years. You ladies helped me pick up the pieces of my life and made me the woman I am today. I'm okay. I'm glad he's been able to move on with his life. That's the way it should be. And other than seeing him at church," I shrugged my shoulders, "I doubt I'll come in much contact with him." Did I really believe what I had just said? My favorite saying came into play right about then.

"After all, with God and chocolate, I can get through anything."

After a busy day consisting of bible study, mystery boxes, an out-of-the-blue announcement, along with the normal hustle and bustle that comes with running a shop, I was wiped out.

Since closing the store at six at night, I wasn't able to stop dreaming of a hot bubble bath. Three hours later, I was just walking through my front door, and that dream would soon be a reality.

I had full intentions of ignoring messages on my phone. I was tired, and drained, and all I wanted was to soak in hot water, read a good book and fall fast asleep. Whoever wanted to talk to me knew to call the shop if it was important enough. And since it wasn't, it would wait until the morning.

Those were my intentions.

The water was running, bubbles had been added, and the book had been selected. That notification of a missed call bothered me more than it should have. Who would have called and left a message? Why not text?

At the first sound of her voice, of course, I knew who wouldn't text. My mother.

I loved my mom, don't get me wrong. But for the past three years, she centered her life around her single daughter who should have been married with children by now. I was her number one priority and it was a pain in the butt.

Even though I lived across town, only a fifteen-minute drive from where I grew up, my mom had a tendency to crowd me. She didn't like the fact I lived alone. She was proud of me for opening my own store, and the fact that it was successful blows both her and dad away.

But that wasn't the trajectory she'd planned out for my life and so she worried and fussed for absolutely no reason. It wasn't like I planned on staying single for the rest of my life.

It wasn't my chosen way of living, let me tell you.

So with a sigh of exasperation, I listened to the message.

"Wynne dear, this is Mom" (as if I didn't recognize her voice). "Listen, I ran into Nancy Montgomery today. She told me the news. Jude is back in town. Isn't that wonderful, honey? You just haven't been the same since he left town" (no Mom, I've actually learned to be independent), "and I know that you both have a lot to catch up on. Listen, I want to invite him over to dinner this week. He was, after all, part of our family for such a long time. Tell me what night is good for you, and I'll make all the arrangements. Maybe you could even bring over one of those cakes you make to sell in your store? Hmmm? Okay, call me back. Love you." Click.

She had no idea. Following the ruination of my wedding day, I refused to talk about it with her or my father. I asked them to respect my privacy and my decision. And that's how it was left. But to invite him to dinner? Knowing how emotionally hurt and physically drained I was when he left, she actually wanted me to share one of my cakes with him?

No where in the bible did it say I had to share my chocolate cake with my enemies – only, that I had to pray for them.

Despite having my own chocolate cafe, there was certain chocolate items I didn't share with just anyone. This was where I drew the line. That was definitely a phone call I just didn't need to hear.

To me, having a bath is a luxury one must never give up. To sink into the hot water, as it completely engulfed you, well, as far as I was concerned, that was close to heaven.

Add scented bubbles, candles all through the room, a cool drink to refresh yourself with, and of course, a little bit of chocolate to nibble on, it couldn't get any better.

It was the one part of my daily routine that I refused to give up. Having a hot bath was not only considered a way to pamper yourself, but it also helped you to fall asleep faster.

Add a good book, and you were off to faraway places, distant lands, and pure romance. That was if your mind behaved itself and went along with your plans.

That night my mind and thoughts decided to rebel.

All I could think about was that Jude was back in town. I would find myself smiling and giving those little happy sighs when I thought of all the great memories we had. And then, I would remember what occurred three years ago and begin to feel anger.

Anger that was first directed toward God and then at myself. Why? Why now? I thought I'd laid it at the foot of the cross and it would no longer be an issue.

So why was it still…an obvious thorn in my side?

I wouldn't allow myself to dwell on my feelings toward God, after all, who could be mad at God? That was just not allowed.

But why, then, when I was happy and contented with my life, did Jude have to come back and remind me of my past failures?

We were just one of those couples who didn't make it. It happened to a lot of people in relationships.

Sometimes you were blessed to have that one deep love, and other times you had to settle for second best. We both decided not to settle.

It would have been nice if we could have kept in touch, but I understood that it would have been difficult for him. Plus, he'd already moved on with his life. That fact alone should have made me happy for him. After all, we were all grown adults. Time had gone by, and while feelings might still be there, there was no possibility of them being acted upon.

My bath was ruined, and I didn't enjoy my small piece of chocolate and the book – I don't think I got past the first page.

I headed to the kitchen to heat water for some gourmet hot chocolate. While waiting for the water to boil, I quickly checked my phone.

I made the mistake of looking at my text messages, though. Not only did Mom call, but she sent me a text too.

> Did you get my message?

> Yes.

> Why didn't you call back?

> Was I supposed to?

> What date is good for dinner?

> I don't want to do dinner, Mom. Sorry

> I thought it was a great idea. To get you and Jude together?

> I don't want to get together, Mom. Please leave it alone.

> I don't understand you. Why won't you tell me what happened? It's not too late you know.

> Yes, it is too late. Good night Mom.

I supposed if I had explained it all to my parents at the time when he left, this would have been avoided. But knowing my parents, they would have tried to fix the problem.

Some problems aren't meant to be fixed.

With a sigh, I fixed my cup of hot chocolate and headed to the living room, where I planned to shut down my thoughts and relax in front of the television, watching either a mindless comedy or a popular drama.

With the fireplace burning and my favorite show about to come on, I settled in for a quiet night of relaxation until the doorbell rang. Seriously. Could I not have a quiet night after having a bit of a stressful day? It had better not be my mother.

I made sure I glanced in the mirror before I opened the door. I was in my pajamas, after all. But I was decent. That's all that mattered. The doorbell rang again. "I'm coming, I'm coming," I called out. I plastered a smile on my face, even though it was the last thing I felt like doing. I opened the door. It was definitely not my mother.

"What are you doing here?" I blurted out.

CHAPTER SIX

mommy dearest

After a busy day consisting of bible study, mystery boxes, an out-of-the-blue announcement, along with the normal hustle and bustle that comes with running a shop, I was wiped out.

Since closing the store at 6 p.m., I wasn't able to stop dreaming of a hot bubble bath. Three hours later, I was just walking through my front door, and that dream would soon be a reality. I had full intentions of ignoring the beeping and flashing light on my answering machine. I was tired, drained and all I wanted was to soak in hot water, read a good book and go off to bed. Whoever wanted to talk to me could have called the shop if it was important enough. And since it wasn't, it can wait until the morning.

Those were my intentions. The water was running, bubbles had been added and the book had been selected. But of course, I needed to check the phone first. You just never know who could have called. It's not like I was expecting anyone from the past to mysteriously drop by, which I wasn't, in case you were wondering. I clicked the button and discovered that I could have resisted the machine after all. It was only my mother.

I love my mom, don't get me wrong. But for the past three years she has been 'concerned' that her daughter has chosen the life of "single hood" rather than motherhood. Even though I live across town, only a fifteen minute drive from where I grew up, my mom has a tendency to crowd me. She doesn't like the fact I live alone. She's proud of me for opening my own store and the fact that it's successful blows both her and dad away. But it's not what she wanted for my life, and so she feels she needs to worry about me. It's not like I plan on staying single for the rest of my life. It's not my chosen way of living let me tell you.

So with a sigh of exasperation, I listened to the message.

"Wynne dear, this is Mom" (as if I didn't recognize her voice). "Listen, I ran into Nancy Montgomery today. She told me the news. Jude is back in town. Isn't that wonderful, honey? You just haven't been the same since he left town" (no Mom, I've actually learned to be independent), "and I know that you both have a lot to catch up on. Listen, I want to invite him over to dinner this week. He was, after all, part of our family for such a long time. Tell me what night is good for you, and I'll make all the arrangements. Maybe you could even bring over one of those cakes you make to sell in your store? Hmmm? Okay, call me back. Love you." Click.

She has no idea. When it all had happened, I refused to talk about it with her or my father. I asked them to respect my privacy and my decision. And that's how it's been left. But to invite him to dinner? Knowing how emotionally hurt and physically drained I was when he left, she actually wants me to share one of my cakes with him? Nowhere in the bible does it say I have to share my chocolate cake with my enemies – only, that I have to pray for them. I don't share my chocolate with just anybody, you know. This is where I draw the line. I shook my head as I headed back to my bath. That was definitely a phone call I just didn't need to hear.

To me, having a bath is a luxury one must never give up. To sink into the hot water, have it completely engulf you, well as far as I'm concerned, this is close to heaven. Add scented bubbles, candles all through the room, a cool drink to refresh yourself with and of course a little bit of chocolate to nibble on, it couldn't get any better. It's the one part of my daily routine that I refuse to give up. Having a hot bath is not only considered a way to pamper yourself, but it also helps you to fall asleep faster. Add a good book, and you're off to far away places, distant lands, and pure romance. That is, if your mind behaves itself and goes along with your plans.

That night my mind and thoughts decided to rebel. All I could think about was that Jude was back in town. I would find myself smiling and giving those little happy sighs when I thought of all the great memories we had. And then, all of a sudden, I would remember what occurred three years ago, and I would begin to feel anger. Anger that was first directed towards God and then at myself. This was something I had already dealt with; it wasn't supposed to hurt me anymore. I laid it at the foot of the cross, and Jesus was supposed to hear all my heart's cries and rescue me. So why wasn't that happening? I won't allow myself to dwell on my feelings towards God, after all, who can be mad at God? That's just not allowed. But why then, when I was happy and contented with my life, did Jude have to come back and remind me of my past failures?

We were just one of those couples who didn't make it. It happens to a lot of people in relationships. Sometimes you are blessed to have that one deep love, and other times you have to settle for second best. We both decided not to settle. It would have been nice if we could have kept in touch, but I understand that it would have been difficult for him. Plus, from what I understood from Nancy, he'd already moved on with his life. That fact alone should have made me happy for him. After all, we were all grown adults. Time had gone by, and while feelings might still be there, there was no possibility of them being acted upon.

My bath was ruined, I didn't enjoy my small piece of chocolate and the book – I don't think I got past the first page. I headed to the kitchen to heat water for some gourmet hot chocolate. While waiting for the water to boil, I quickly checked my email. Perhaps

I should unplug the phone just in case mommy dearest decided to call back. I definitely was not in the mood for a conversation with her tonight.

Too late. My phone dings with a text message from her:

MOM2CHOCQUEN (MOM TO CHOCOLATE QUEEN).

MM2CHOCQUEN: Did you get my message?

CHOCQUEEN: Yes.

MM2CHOCQUEN: Why didn't you call back?

CHOCQUEEN: Was I supposed to?

MM2CHOCQUEN: What date is good for dinner?

CHOCQUEEN: I don't want to do dinner Mom. Sorry

MM2COCQUEN: I thought it was a great idea. To get you and Jude together?

CHOCQUEEN: I don't want to get together Mom. Please leave it alone.

MM2COCQUEN: I don't understand you. Why won't you tell me what happened? It's not too late you know.

CHOCQUEEN: Yes, it is too late. Good night Mom.

I suppose if I had explained it all to my parents at the time when he left, this could have been avoided. But knowing my parents, they would have tried to fix the problem. This was just one problem that could not be fixed.

With a sigh, I shut down my computer, fixed my cup of hot chocolate, and headed to the living room, where I planned to shut down my thoughts and relax in front of the television watching either a mindless comedy or a popular drama.

With the fireplace turned on, my favorite show about to come on, I settled in for a quiet night of relaxation. Until the doorbell rang. Seriously. Could I not have a quiet night after having a bit of a stressful day? It had better not be my mother.

I made sure I glanced in the mirror before I opened the door. I was in my pyjamas, after all. But I was decent. That's all that mattered. The doorbell rang again. "I'm coming, I'm coming," I called out. I plastered a smile on my face, even though it was the last thing I felt like doing. I opened the door. It was definitely not my mother.

"What are you doing here?" I blurted out.

CHAPTER SEVEN

the other woman

"What do you mean, what am I doing here? Is that how you greet your best friend? What do you think I'm doing here?" Heather said. "Our program is on and I brought some munchies. Now get out of the doorway so I can come in before we miss too much."

"Sorry. I forgot about tonight." I tried to apologize as I followed behind her to the couch.

"You had better be sorry. I made a batch of my famous chewy chocolate chip cookies and ruffled plain chips with dip. But if you keep up with the attitude, I'll just keep the cookies to myself." Heather held the bag in front of my nose and teased me mercilessly.

"Oh, you're so tough. Give me those." I made a grab for the cookies and managed to snatch them from her greedy fingers. Imagine the audacity of threatening me with cookies.

About halfway through the program, I decided to broach the subject that I knew Heather actually wanted to talk about.

"So, I guess you heard the news about today?"

"Whew. It's about time you brought it up. I've been impatiently waiting all evening to talk to you about it. How are you doing? Oh, off subject, what did you think of the Sweet Surprise boxes?" Heather asked.

"Hmmm, I loved them. You did an amazing job creating those little chocolate baskets with all the little goodies. Just perfect. I think we should do more of those throughout the year, but I'll order some boxes with windows, so you can see the baskets. You once again outdid yourself. Thank you."

I seriously loved all her creations. I sincerely believed her gift was with food. Not one single thing that she made turned out tasting bad. Me, on the other hand, well, let's just say that I'm not that gifted in the area of cooking. Now baking, that is a different story. Where do you think all the cakes in my store came from?

"Thanks. That's a great idea. I'll have to charge extra next time," Heather said with a wink.

"Listen, with all that you do, I couldn't even begin to repay you. As Matt says, you're worth your weight in gold.

"But, in all seriousness, I'm okay. Can you imagine Nancy coming up to me like that and telling me to stay away from her son? The claws were visible this time around. She reminded me of a mother bear with her cub. Do I look that dangerous?

"After everything, does she really think we would pick up right where we left off? Um, hello. Besides, from what I understood, he's already involved, and more than likely hasn't given me one moment of his thoughts. But why should he? He's the one who ran away rather than face the music and try to work things out." I babbled. It almost sounded like it mattered to me, after all this time.

"Methinks the lady doth protest too much," said Heather.

"Hmm, it sounds that way, doesn't it? But it doesn't matter, though, does it?" I said, with a hint of sadness starting to settle in. Did I allow my heart hurts to surface, or did I shrug them off again and pretend it didn't bother me?

With Heather, I didn't have to worry about hiding things. And even if I did, she knew me too well. She knew the whole story, after all.

"Wynne, I really think it would be helpful if you talked to Jude about it. Bring it out in the open and face the issues. It doesn't matter if it's in the past; it's a part of who you are. You need closure. Then you'll feel free to move on with your life. You guys made the right decision, so stop beating yourself up about it. It's time you invested some time into a man, into your future, something other than Chocolate Blessings," encouraged Heather.

"Hmmm, we'll have to see. Right now, I don't think it would make much difference. We're one of those casual acquaintances that have a bit of history. We'll be the type of people who are able to say hi without too much awkwardness," I said without too much conviction.

"Well, I'm sure it will all work out. You might even be a bit surprised at the outcome. I'm here for you nonetheless. Anyway, I've been thinking. We need to plan a girls' night out. I think Tracey could really use it, and it's been a while since we've done anything fun." Heather said while grabbing another cookie.

"Good idea. Where should we go? How about Mama Rose's? Or grab a chick flick at the theater? Do you think we can convince Tracey to join us? Last time we tried to plan a girls' night, she canceled on us at the last minute." I said.

After Tracey's last baby, it seems like she's had a hard time finding enjoyment in life. Having three children has to be tiring, but it seems to be more than that. A couple of months ago, Heather and I had the brilliant idea that Tracey needed to have a night with no kids. We planned a dinner and shopping spree. At the last minute, Tracey canceled, using the excuse that the baby was being fussy and she didn't feel right leaving him with Mike.

"Matt has already spoken with Mike, and he's working on clearing a night from his calendar so that he can be home with the kids. As soon as he lets us know, we'll go and literally kidnap Tracey so that she doesn't have time to think of an excuse," Heather plotted.

I giggled. "Ohhh, you sound so sinister."

Heather shook her head as she gathered her things together.

"Now, it's time to go home. I'll let you keep the few cookies that are left. Don't think about Jude too much tonight - okay, Wynne? No sense worrying about something you can't handle until it's hitting you in the face. I'll be in the store tomorrow, so I'll see you then," said Heather.

Don't think too much about Jude? Who was she kidding? That was all I was going to think about - him and our past together. For three years I'd successfully brushed it all to the side, locked in a little box within my mind, and went on with my life.

Don't think too much about it?

Dear Diary, here I come.

chewy chocolate chip cookies

Who doesn't like cookies...especially chewy chocolate chip cookies!

My husband complains I don't make these enough, but there's a reason for that...unlike Wynne who seems to eat all the chocolate and desserts she wants without it affecting the waistline...I would eat them all and never share :)

CHEWY CHOCOLATE CHIP COOKIES

INGREDIENTS:

- 1 cup butter (softened)
- 1 cup sugar
- 3/4 cup brown sugar
- 2 large eggs
- 2 tsp vanilla
- 2 cups flour
- 1 tsp baking soda
- 1/4 tsp sale
- Bag of chocolate chips (or 1 1/2 cups)

STEPS:

1. Preheat oven to 350
2. In a large bowl, beat butter and sugars until pale and light.
3. Beat in the eggs and vanilla.
4. Add flour, baking soda and sale and stir until combined.
5. Add the chocolate chips - as many as you want.
6. Drop the dough by large spoonfuls, spacing a couple inches (they will spread) on parchment lined cookie sheet.
7. Bake for 15 min (until golden brown)
8. Transfer to cooking rack and WAIT for at least a few seconds before you eat them…don't burn your lips or tongue on the hot chocolate chips!

Everyone has a cookie recipe they love. These ones are thin and chewy and OH SO GOOD! I swear it's the brown sugar and vanilla…but it could really be anything.

Enjoy and yes, you'll probably want to eat them all. I know I always do.

CHAPTER EIGHT

pass the coffee

I glanced out the window to see the sun shining and snow glistening like sparkling diamonds, children laughing as they built snowmen, and saw the thermometer outside my window reading a balmy –18. Brrrrrrrr. Why was it that children never seem to mind the cold while adults always dreaded it?

I bundled up nice and warm with a thick sweater, my parka, wooly mitts, scarf, and hat, grabbed the chocolate cake that I finished making early this morning, and headed out to my car.

The whole way down the stairs and across the walkway, I found myself saying a double prayer. "Lord, please let my car start this morning, please let me make it to my car without falling." I should have been wearing my ice skates, either that or skiing down the path to my car.

If I could make it in one piece this morning without the cake becoming an upside-down creation, I'd be happy.

I start to bargain with God, if I could just make it in one piece, I promised to smile at all those I met, even though my lips might crack due to the cold, I will play Christmas music all day, and I'll even make chocolate chip cookies for my next-door neighbor who gives me all those mean looks when I come home late in the evening and put on my favorite worship CD.

Please and Amen.

I loved the routine of opening up the store. I got to see the store in its glory, quiet, clean, and well-stocked, just waiting for customers to come in and fall in love with all the delicious treats.

When the first aroma of coffee began to drift through the store, then I knew it was time to open. I decided long ago, that no customer would walk into our store and not be greeted by the fresh aroma of brewed coffee and chocolate.

I mean, who in their right mind could start their day without those essentials?

I liked to have a Flavor of the Week, something that was a new creation for me. I also sold it as a ready-made beverage. That week I decided to make Dreamy Swiss Mocha Coffee Mix.

I'd hit the jackpot last summer when I discovered boxes of decorative tins at a flea market in a nearby town. I'd been using those tins for an assortment of gift ideas ever since.

The current plan for the tins was to hold the dry mix of Dreamy Swiss Mocha Coffee. Add some ribbon, a little card detailing instructions on how to make the coffee, and voila. The perfect gift.

For the store, I liked to prepare it in a large slow cooker and have it simmering all day. I offered this free, as a taste test to indulge the senses. I found it to be a great selling feature.

As I was getting the cake I made last night ready for display, my first customer walked through the door.

First customers were treated special in my store. They always got the first slice of cake along with a rose, free of charge. The policy had gotten around a bit, and oftentimes I'd find a lineup of people waiting for me to open the door.

"Good morning. Thank you for coming in this morning. I have a fresh pot of Swiss Mocha on this morning, please help yourself."

I called out as a greeting. I didn't recognize the woman who walked in, so I knew she wasn't a regular.

"I noticed your store last night as we drove into town. I love gourmet coffee, and when I saw your sign, I knew this would be the perfect place to come for my coffee," my guest gave me a brief smile as she walked through the store and examined all the displays and hangings on the walls.

"There is a little corner where the coffee is so you can relax and enjoy your morning treat," I said as I continued to set up the cake. I took a few peeks at the tall, blonde, and really quite beautiful woman.

As my guest walked through the store, in walked Tracey sans her children. You could tell she was in the "get me away" mode, for as soon as she walked in, she took a deep breath, and a sigh of relief escaped her mouth at the same time.

"Hey, lady. You look like you need a strong cup of coffee and a special treat to go with it. How about a lemon poppy seed muffin?" I suggested with a smile on my face. She really did look like she needed to get away for a while.

"Wynne. My angel in disguise. Would you mind if I took my muffin, coffee, and book and curled myself up in one of your comfy chairs for, oh, I don't know, a few years? Perhaps even decades?" Tracey shook her head as she poured her coffee.

"Um, no, but I might need to start charging you a sitting fee. Go on over, and enjoy some quiet. I'll come over in a bit and join you for coffee."

"Thanks so much. You're a sweetie. But just to warn you … give me a good half hour or more before you come over. I need that much time just to cool down," she warned as she headed over to the comfy section of the café.

Tracey and I had been friends forever. I was there when she first met Mike, her husband. At the time, she was adamant about never marrying a pastor. I think we were both of the same mind. I mean, who would actually want to be married to a man who had to spend more time at the church than at his own home? If he didn't, the "sheep" complained?

Being a pastor wasn't a Sunday morning preaching from the pulpit kind of job. It was preaching three different sermons each week, plus, counseling parishioners, making hospital visits, home visits and so much more.

It was exhausting, just thinking about it. I remember watching our senior pastor's wife while I grew up. I always thought that not only did she marry the pastor, but she also married the ministry and all the headaches associated with it.

It would take a special person to do that, and neither Tracey nor I figured we could do it.

Growing up, Tracey was the best of the two of them. She was smart, challenging, fun, strong, and always had a goal set out before her. She challenged me and was my best friend.

Besties forever.

We made a pact that we would be one of those women who changed the world, not have the world change them. We were going to conquer all that came our way.

Someone had once suggested that we both go to Bible College, to get some good training on how to be a perfect wife. Can you imagine the audacity?

Instead, I went to college and took English literature. Tracey went on to become an accountant. Blah and boring, you might think, but she is a whiz when it comes to numbers. In her second last year, she met Mike at a church service.

Long story short, they fell in love, she left me to marry him, never finished her degree, and instead began to have babies.

When she met Mike, he was finishing his degree at Bible College and had high aspirations of changing today's youth. Despite all our vows, Tracey became that dreaded pastor's wife. She was happy, though. Surprisingly, motherhood fulfilled a dream within her heart that neither one of us knew she had.

Throughout the past few years, she has had more babies, three in total, and I have watched her slowly fall into a depression. It was more than the baby blues, but anytime I brought it up, she shut me down quick.

While I was dwelling on my good friend, my unknown customer walked up to the counter. She beamed me a smile that I just couldn't help but return.

"Wynne, is it?" There was a lyrical tone to her voice, sweet almost. I nodded.

"What a cute store. Perhaps you can help me a little?" she asked while she turned her gaze to the floor and began to fidget a little bit with her hands.

"I am a guest in someone's home, and I would like to buy her a gift. I'm having a hard time choosing, and was hoping that you might be familiar with her."

"Not a problem. Perhaps if you told me her name, we can figure out something for her together," I suggested while she gave me a sheepish look.

"Oh sure, I, um, thought you would have known. Sorry. It's Mrs. Montgomery, Jude's mother."

My jaw dropped. I'm sure of it.

"Of course, I know Nancy. She was just in here yesterday to tell me Jude was coming home. I'm sorry, I didn't catch your name?" Did that come out too harsh? Too abrupt?

"I'm Stacey. Stacey Lawd. Jude mentioned that you owned a store, but I didn't realize it was this one," she said a bit apologetically

Wait...so she wouldn't have come in if she actually knew that this was my store?

"I passed by on my walk this morning and just had to stop in. Do you think you can help me find a gift? I think it's safe to assume that you know Nancy a bit better than I do." She suddenly turned a nice shade of pink.

While Stacey was mentioning her quest for that perfect gift for Nancy, I couldn't help but notice the absence of a ring on her finger. Ah, the awkwardness of getting to know the parents. She must still have been in the stages of getting Nancy to like her. I felt for her. It could be quite a daunting task. I was once in her shoes, so I should know.

"Tell you what," I continued. "Let's just get all the awkwardness out of the way, shall we? I was once engaged to Jude, broke his heart, he left town, and that is all in the past. I'm assuming you are his girlfriend, and it must be serious if he brought you home. Since we have so much in common, let's use that as our common purpose and not allow all the other garbage to get in the way."

I couldn't believe I just said that. Talk about bold and daring. But one thing I have learned over the years, if you use honesty to your advantage, you can never go wrong.

In this case, I figured that if I'd never met a chocolate I didn't like, that also had to be true for friends. Besides, if I just assumed everyone I met would become a good friend, then how could I go wrong?

"That's a relief, I was a bit nervous, if you couldn't tell, about meeting you," Stacey said.

Instead of the awkwardness that surrounded us earlier, it now felt the opposite. She seemed like she was a breath of fresh air. I was already beginning to like her.

"Hmm…well, she loves chocolate, stationery, and candles." I listed off a few suggestions to her, hoping that she would have already noticed a few items that caught her eye.

"What about some of those wall wreaths? Or do you think that might be too inappropriate for right now?" Stacey asked.

"Hmm, I have noticed her admiring them before, but, and this is just my personal suggestion, how about doing up a little basket with a few things in it? That way, it's not too overpowering, and you know she will fawn over it all. We have some vintage milk candlesticks or vases, a few votives, a pad of stationery, and perhaps a tea towel for the kitchen. Or it could be a themed basket?" I suggested. I had a few more customers walk into the store, and I needed to focus some attention on them.

"I love the idea of a themed basket. I'll just take a look around, and let you get back to work. Thanks, Wynne," Stacey said as she walked away.

I had to admit that Stacey didn't seem too bad. I don't know what I was expecting. In my head, I visualized the 'unknown' lady friend coming up to me and giving me a good ole' chick slap, right across my face, in revenge for hurting her dearly beloved. She would walk away with refined dignity, and I would be left standing there, with a red cheek, feeling utter amazement and embarrassment. Not a pretty sight, and definitely, not the type of daydream that I like to have.

It would have been nice to be left in la-la land for a little while, just me and my thoughts and weird daydreams, but I was rudely brought out of my reverie by an insistent voice mentioning my chocolate cake.

"Wynne, the perfect sight for the perfect morning. Look at that cake you made. It looks absolutely delicious. Do you think it's too early to have a slice now? Oh, and see the pretty little pink rose-buds. I would have to say that the cake-decorating course you took last year has definitely paid off. A beautiful showcase. Oh, and I'll definitely plan on enjoying your Dreamy Swiss Mocha. Of course, I will take some of that too. Wherever did you find those tins? I love them. I think you should create a display of them and sell them. They would definitely be a hot item around here. You just know how much everyone loves these cute tins. Antique, aren't they? I think my mother used to have a bunch of these when I was just a wee little lass. Now those were the days. No frills, just plain honest hard work, and simplicity. That's what got us through the day. But then, I wasn't allowed to have chocolate for breakfast either … so on that note, I think I will have a slice of your cake." Slightly out of breath, Joan beamed a huge smile.

"Sometimes, it's really hard to keep up with you." I couldn't help but giggle just a teenie little bit.

"As for the tins, I found them at a garage sale. Aren't they darling? Tell you what, just because you are my favorite customer, how about an extra big slice of cake?" I like to spoil

Joan. Sometimes it doesn't always hurt to treat someone as if they were just a little extra special, especially when it happens to be true.

"Well, thank you, my dear girl. You certainly know how to make one's day. Now, I do believe that is Tracey I see over there sitting by herself this morning. I think she needs a good ole mama hug. Don't you be shaking your head at me. You can see that she is one hurting girl, and when the Lord told me to come over here this morning, I knew it was for a reason. That girl over there just needs to be reminded that she is loved." With that, Joan took off over to Tracey.

Joan was one of those sweet women who go about each day fully trusting in God to lead her. She believed that God ordered the steps of a righteous woman, and she was determined to walk each step the way God would have her.

Where I tended just to stand back and give people space when they asked for it, Joan will just walk right into that space that they hold onto so dearly and hug them.

She had powerful hugs.

Stacey walked over to the counter with her arms full of items for her basket. I casually went through what she had picked, and I had to admit, she had excellent taste. She went with a Kitchen theme. Hand soap, tarts, a tart burner, kitchen-scented candles, homespun tea towels, a little plaque that has embroidered "Give us this day our daily bread" within it, a coffee mug, a white water pitcher, and a box of chocolates.

"I like your selections, Stacey. I think she will definitely like what you picked out. Would you like me to wrap it up?" I asked.

She shrugged her dainty shoulders. "Thanks. I hope she likes it all, and yes, could you wrap it up for me?"

I turn my back to select a big enough basket, when the bell over the door rang. I was just about to turn when I heard his voice.

"There you are. I thought maybe you had gotten lost on your walk, and I came to find you. I almost didn't notice you from the window. Are you ready to go?" The voice belonged to, yep, you guessed it. Jude.

I took a deep breath before I turned. That was not how I wanted to see Jude for the first time in over three years.

In my mind, it played out that I might see him from a distance at church, or maybe walking down the street. We would casually say hi, how are you, nice to see you again and continue on our way.

I, of course, would look great, with my hair all done up nice, fresh lipstick on, and clothes to show that I had lost weight since he was last here.

Why couldn't life actually be like my dreams?

"Hey," we both said in unison. Well, wasn't that awkward?

He looked great. Tall, and slender but his shoulders were broader than I remembered. He must have been working out. He still had those soft blue eyes that just made a girl want to daydream.

He looked great in his tan sweater with dark blue jeans. He was obviously still impartial to the cold weather since he had his coat slung over his arm. Where most people would be bundled up since it is winter, Jude used to just walk around in a thick sweater with a scarf wrapped around him.

His arm was across Stacey's shoulder as if he was trying to show that he was taken, like that would really matter to me. They looked great together, though.

I gave a wistful sigh and realized with a jolt that he was still talking to me while I was daydreaming. Again.

"Welcome home," I said. To make it appear like I did actually hear him, I threw out my arms in a wide arc. In the process of doing this, I remembered that I had just finished arranging a display of tins with the Swiss Mocha right beside me on the top of the display counter.

Before I could even begin to stop myself, my one arm swept across the display case, catching the tins in the process. While I was slowly moaning 'oh no', I watched the tins as if in slow motion, topple from the counter onto the floor. One decided to become aerobic and bounced from the top of the pile, onto the counter, and then onto me. The bounce from the counter caused the lid to come off, allowing the mocha mix to escape the tin and converge onto my new black sweater.

Great, just great.

I heaved a big sigh while trying to smile and not look embarrassed at the same time. I decided to take the graceful way out, and handed Stacey her bag, praying fervently under my breath that they would leave. Soon, like as in now.

Jude laughed. Stacey giggled. I just stood there, slightly dazed, when the humor of the whole thing finally hit me. I joined in the laughing. From the corner, I heard Joan yelling "she's at it again," and from that moment on, I was lost.

I grabbed the edge of the counter, I was laughing so hard. An awkward situation became humorous. It was all at my expense, but then, what else was new?

"It's nice to know not all things have changed," Jude managed to utter in between his laughs. He took Stacey's bag and led her to the front door. As they walked, Stacey called out from over her shoulder.

"Wynne, it was nice meeting you. Thanks for all your help," she said as she waved her purse in the air. And with that, they left me standing there, not believing what had just occurred.

CHAPTER NINE

the kick in the gut

There was a message on my phone that I'd been ignoring for past hour or so.

Why? No idea.

It was from Tracey, but after the day I had, there was a part of me that wanted to hibernate for the rest of the year.

"Hey girl, it's Friday night, kids are in bed, Mike is working on a sermon, and I'm in the mood for a chick flick. If I bring the movie and popcorn, will you supply the chocolate and blankets? Give me a call when you get in."

Okay, that wasn't too bad.

Watching a chick flick with a girlfriend was an excellent way to end the horrible day I had. After Jude and Stacey left the store, I had to endure teasing from Judy and Tracey. It was bad enough that I felt utterly embarrassed, but to listen to others enjoy my humiliation was more than I could handle.

After about ten minutes of their teasing, and repeating the story to new customers as they walked in, I ordered those two wisecrackers out of my store. I threatened to banish them if they repeated the story of my humiliation to one more person.

I wasn't sure if it worked or not, since they ended up leaving the store with tears of laughter rolling down their faces, but at least I felt better.

All day I had people who I thought were my friends come into the store. Not to offer me sympathy, but wanting more details.

I don't understand people. The man I was about to marry, but ended up breaking his heart, finally came back into town after three years. My first time seeing him included having to meet his new girlfriend and making a complete fool of myself - and they thought that was gossip worthy?

That being said, I did end up selling a lot since I made everyone who needled me for details buy something, whether it be chocolate, candles, or coffee.

After a long and tiring day, I just wanted to go home and relax. Between everyone either coming into the store or blowing up my phone until I just turned it off, it's been quite the day.

But, that's small-town life for you. No one was a stranger, and you always knew when someone sneezed.

Before Tracey came, I decided to indulge and make a pan of hot fudge brownies. These were my absolute favorite, and something that I never made for the store.

I only shared them with a few sacred friends. It had been a while since Tracey and I had one of those good ole chick nights, so I figured this was a special enough occasion to indulge ourselves.

With the Pina Colada mix ready and the beeper on my oven about to go off, the doorbell rang.

"Come on in," I yelled. "I'm in the kitchen." The beeper on the oven went off, so I heard a voice calling to me, but couldn't quite understand the words.

"You're just in time. Our drink is ready, and the brownies are fresh out of the oven warm. Now, all we need is the popcorn, and our chick night can begin. What movie did you bring?" My back was turned to the doorway. I had my flannel pajamas on, with my "I'm so sexy" apron on and my big fuzzy pink princess slippers. With it being girls' night, flannel and fuzzy slippers only seemed appropriate.

"Hmm, I don't think a chick night is exactly my thing, but thanks anyway."

I froze. That voice did not belong to sweet, feminine Tracey. Instead, it was a deep and definitely masculine Jude.

Once again, this was not the way that I wanted to see him. Not in flannels, apron, and slippers. Not with me bending over my stove door, face flushed.

I straightened up slowly, carefully placed the brownies onto my counter, and tried to halfway compose myself.

"Um, no. Chick night definitely would not suit you. Sorry, I um, thought you were Tracey," I apologized. Talk about embarrassment. If a hole could have materialized and swept me out of the kitchen right then, I'd have claimed it a miracle.

"This is a nice place you have, Wynne. It feels homey, and, well, you. It seems like you created what you always desired – a home," said Jude while he glanced around my kitchen/dining area.

"Um, thanks?" Small talk with an ex-fiance was difficult.

I was able to buy my dream home a few years ago. It was an older style home, complete with hardwood floors, old wood details around the door frames and windows, old furnace heaters in every room, and wood sliding doors between my living room and dining area. It was a bit run down when I bought it, thus enabling me to get a good deal, but with a lot of work, it's everything I'd ever imagined.

I've decorated it with sparse decor, semi-embracing the hygge movement. Minimalist Scandinavian with a touch of shabby chic. It doesn't suit everyone's taste, but I loved it. And it didn't hurt that a lot of my accessories came from my store, either.

"So Jude, what brings you by? Where is Stacey? Does she trust you alone with me?" Okay, okay, there was a bit of sarcasm in that last comment. I should have apologized, but I wouldn't.

"Be nice. I thought we should talk. Stacey knows where I am and why. I left her with mom going through those dreaded photo albums that all mothers seem to bring out at the wrong times. I needed to get out and thought to come over here. I hope you don't mind me not calling first. Although," and he was looking me up and down when he said this, "maybe I should have called first."

Ya, think?

"Hey – it's not my fault you caught me like this, and there's nothing wrong with how I'm dressed. Tracey is coming by, and we're having a girls' night. Sorry, but no boys allowed," I answered back.

"All right, I won't stay, but can you spare a few moments to talk? There's something I want to tell you, and I thought you should hear it from me first."

Oh no. Those dreaded words. He was going to tell me he was engaged. I just knew it. And why it bothered me, I'm not sure, but it did. It did a lot.

"I plan on asking Stacey to marry me tonight. I thought that with all that we have been through, you deserved to hear it from me first."

There was my answer.

It hurt. I masked my face so that it didn't show. I took a deep breath and plastered the largest smile I'd ever had to fake onto my face.

"Congratulations. Wow. I'm … happy for you Jude. That's great. Stacey seems like a great person, and, well, I'm happy for you." Call me the queen of fakeness.

"Are you really? I know it shouldn't matter, but it does. Part of me feels bad for finally having found someone I love with all my heart, while you are still, well, you're still here. Waiting." Jude twiddled his fingers.

Ouch. I felt like I'd been kicked in the gut by a sumo wrestler.

"I just wanted, no, I needed, well - I'm not sure why I wanted you to know first. I know we once had something special, but I couldn't stand knowing that I would always take second place in your heart. I finally realized what you meant by not taking second best. We would have been good for each other, but you're right.

We would have been settling." Jude walked across the length of my kitchen and back again.

Was I supposed to answer? Did he want me to agree with him?

"I don't feel I'm settling with Stacey. She's the absolute best. I love her. I hope you can be happy for me?" Jude looked at me with those big puppy dog eyes. I never could refuse him anything when he looked at me that way.

"Of course, I'm happy for you. She must be very special to have claimed your heart, Jude. I'm happy for you." Didn't I just say that? "I'll admit it's a hard pill to swallow. You are going to have what I always dreamed of having."

I felt the tears well up in my eyes. "I think I always thought that once I could let go of the past, once I gave up that dream I have, you would be the one to have me with open arms. I am happy for you. You're moving on with your life while I'm stuck living in the past." I replied as honesty as I could before I turned away to hide my tears.

Jude placed his arms around me a gave me a hug. I stiffened up; after all, it's been three years since I was last in this position. But I gradually began to feel safe and let myself relax a bit as tears continued to run down my face. It felt nice to be in a man's arms again, even if he wasn't my man.

I took a big breath and gently stepped away from the embrace. It was a good thing I did, for at the same time, I heard my front door open and close, with Tracey calling out a greeting as she closed the door.

Jude stepped away slowly until he was back leaning against the kitchen counter. I quickly wiped away my tears and tried to appear busy while I composed myself. With a quick look at Jude, I called out to Tracey.

"In the kitchen." Before I could begin to warn her that Jude was here, Tracey called out while she was walking.

"Hmmm, something smells good. Please tell me you made the..." She faltered as she entered the kitchen. She glanced from me to Jude and back again. "Brownies," she finished a bit lamely.

"Hey, Tracey. Nice to see you again. I just came by to talk with Wynne. But I'll scoot now since I know you guys have other plans that don't include men," greeted Jude as he offered a bit of a goofy smile.

"You're the last person I expected to see today. But hey, nothing about today has gone as planned, so why not. Where's the girlfriend?" She glanced around the kitchen, clearly making a point.

Oh oh, Tracey was in full-blown mother-hen mode. Ruffled feathers and all.

"I ah, er, well, um, at home with my mom. I...I just wanted to chat with Wynne, share some news." Jude stammered.

"And what type of news would that be? Does it affect her at all? And what type of news would you have to share that Stacey couldn't be here ..." Tracey slowly stopped, cluing into what that news could be.

"Yep, you guessed it, Tracey," I began. I decided to try and rescue the situation a bit here.

"Jude is ..."

"I am ..."

We both began and stopped at the same time.

"It's your news Jude, you share it," I offered.

"I am going to ask Stacey to marry me, and I wanted to tell Wynne before she heard it from someone else," Jude explained to Tracey.

"And I'm so thrilled," I injected, "that I'm going to throw them an engagement party." Now, where in the world did that come from? Me and my big mouth.

"You are?" both Jude and Tracey said together, both sounding a little bit shocked.

"I am," I answered with a ring of finality to it. After all, it might be a good decision in the long run. That way none of the busybodies of our town would talk about poor Wynne, the jilted - in their eyes - bride.

"I am. Doesn't that sound like a splendid idea? After all, I love parties, and I love to throw them. Why shouldn't I do this? I want to, plus it will stop all the gossip about my supposedly broken heart if I do this." I said. Okay, so maybe I sounded a bit desperate with my explanation, but there was no way I was going to be talked out of this now.

"Okay," began Tracey with a bit of hesitancy in her voice. "Okay, so you, Jude, are getting married, and you, Wynne, are throwing an engagement party. All right. It sounds a bit … hmm, weird, but then you both were always a bit weird together, so who am I to argue? Congratulations, by the way, Jude." Stacey stopped as she headed towards Jude.

"It is girls' night, Wynne's famous brownies are done, and the smell is calling to me. I think it's time you left, and we'll all deal with," she waved her hands around, "whatever just happened here in the morning." Tracey grabbed his arm and literally pulled him out of my kitchen.

I couldn't move from my spot in the kitchen. Did he really just tell me that he's getting engaged? Had I really just said that I would throw him an engagement party? Was there any possibility that I could be dreaming right then?

I remained in the same spot when Tracey came back into the kitchen. I lifted my head to look her in the eyes. I teared up again, and as she gently enfolded me in her arms, I bawled like a little blubbering baby.

After a few minutes, I composed myself and lifted my head. With a smile on my face, I offered the following suggestion.

"Let's eat the brownies, have our drink, and enjoy our chick night, shall we?"

wynne's decadently delicious hot fudge brownies

The recipe for this comes from my childhood - my best friend and I would always make cookies during our sleepovers - and only leave crumbs for her brother to enjoy :) These really taste good with ice cream on top too!

WYNNE'S DECADENTLY DELICIOUS HOT FUDGE BROWNIES

INGREDIENTS:

- 4 eggs
- 1 1/2 cup sugar
- 1/2 cup brown sugar
- 1/2 cup butter (melted)
- 1 cup cocoa
- 2 tbsp hot fudge sauce (the thicker the better)
- 3 tbsp hot fudge sauce (for the topping)
- 1 tsp vanilla
- 1/2 cup flour

STEPS:

- Preheat oven to 350
- Grease 9x9 pan with butter or spray
- In a large bowl, combine sugar and butter and mix
- Add eggs and vanilla. Mix well.
- Fold in the four and cocoa - mix but don't overmix (if that makes sense…and fold, don't use your stand mixer for this)
- Add in 2 tbsp of lightly warmed hot fudge (20 sec in microwave)
- Mix again
- Pour into the pan and yes, you can lick the bowl!
- Spread the rest of the hot fudge (warmed) across the top of the brownies. I like to make lines and then drag a spoon or knife through the lines.
- Bake until sides have slightly pulled away from the pan (about 20-30 min…all depends on how gooey you want these. If you do the toothpick trick - you don't want it to come out clean).

Top with ice cream or whipped cream (my fav) and even add some more chocolate sauce if you want.

CHAPTER TEN

the past

W e made a pact with one another.

We'd enjoy our movie and snacks before we got into any of the heavy conversations we both knew would follow. As if we could just not talk about what had happened, or the reason why she was not only in the store this morning for a time out, but in addition, here at my house tonight for the same reason.

After refills of our drinks, another plate of brownies and our sanity being satisfied with our chick flick, we both took up opposite sides of the couch and settled in for some interesting girly talk. Up for discussion at this moment was the scene earlier in my kitchen.

"I still say we should have a coin toss for who goes first," I began. I wasn't sure I really wanted to delve into the why's of my reactions just yet. I'd rather have sunk my teeth into what was going on inside Tracey at the moment.

"Don't think I'm going to let you get away with not talking about Jude. Wynne Taylor, I think what happened tonight is a bit more important than the problems I'm having in my marriage. Those will always be there, so it's not all that important," Tracey admonishment kind of stung and I wasn't sure why.

"All right, I'll be the self-sacrificing friend and allow you to dissect me and my reactions. For now, though. Don't think you're getting out of this any time soon, missy," I replied, wiggling my finger in front of her face.

"Should I lie down here while you analyze me?" I stuck my tongue out at her.

"Don't be saucy, or I might just eat up the rest of the brownies. What in all of God's green earth possessed you to agree to hold his engagement party?" A tone of incredibility filled her voice.

"He didn't ask me. I volunteered. And as to why ... I'm not sure exactly, but the more I think about the idea, the more I like it. Come on ... think about it, Tracey. If I do this for them, no one will be able to look at me with pity in their eyes or think I'm just trying to put on a good face rather than show everyone how broken they think my heart truly is. Isn't that perfect or what?" I explained to her.

"Or what. You need to think about this. You almost married that man. I was there, I saw it all. You were wearing your wedding dress, the music was playing, and you were ready to walk down that aisle and become Mrs. Jude Montgomery. Then all of a sudden, poof, there is Jude at the door demanding to speak with you, and he orders all of your good friends, including your bewildered parents, out of the room so the two of you can talk. Next thing we know, we're being told the wedding is off, Jude has split for who knows where, and you are left sitting on the floor in a puddle of tears."

Why did she have to mention that? Why bring up the past when all it did was hurt?

"You expect everyone to be happy and accept that you are throwing him an engagement party. That's not going to fly. Everyone is going to think you're just being the good old Christian martyr that you are, and while you have a good face on, you're crying inside. Come on now, girl," Tracey said.

I tried to look anywhere but at her. What she said made sense.

"Oh, all right," I sighed. "But you are one of the few people who actually know what transpired that day. So you should know that I don't have any feelings for him anymore."

"Do I need to call up Heather and get her to come over and talk some sense into you?" Tracey asked. Heather was the only other person who also knew the details of that day.

"No, you don't need to throw threats around. Jude came into that room to tell me that he couldn't settle for being second best. He finally admitted to himself that my heart still belonged to another. I would have walked down that aisle if he didn't come to the room, you know that, Tracey. I think he just finally realized what I could never tell him. I loved him, but not enough." I rest my head against the couch and let it all sink in. The heartache. The heartbreak. The feeling of being less than, of not being enough. It all came rushing back, and I hated every single moment of it.

"I tried, Tracey, I really did. I tried to let go of my first love; I was determined to be happy with Jude. But I had to be honest when he asked me."

That was the hardest thing I had ever done ... to be completely honest with him. He wanted my whole heart. Since I couldn't give it to him, I ended up breaking his.

"Whatever happened to the happy ever after? I know in my heart that I did the right thing. But I gave up my dreams and desires. So when is it my time, Tracey?" I felt big fat tears roll down my face.

"Am I not good enough for God yet? Or does He have some big purpose for me living the single life? 'Cause if He does, then I wish He would help me to get rid of the dream I have in my heart. Otherwise, it's not fair," I cried out.

That was the first time I'd verbally voiced my feelings to someone other than the walls of my room about this.

Deep in my heart, I felt not only hurt but also betrayed by God. That wasn't something that I was willing to confess on a regular basis. As a Christian, who could honestly say that God betrayed them? That just wasn't right. And I knew deep down it wasn't true.

"My ways are not your ways, nor are my thoughts your thoughts," the Bible said.

I was in love once. I never really fell out of it. I was just too immature to realize what I had. I thought that marriage meant having to sacrifice too much. I was only twenty-three; I believed I had all the time in the world. Plus, I thought that if it were real, the love that we shared, then it would always be there.

So I tested that theory. I was wrong. He walked away, and I let him go.

A few years later, I met Jude. He swept me off my feet and made me laugh. He accepted me for who I was and gave me the courage to dare to dream.

We dated for a few years before Jude confessed his love to me and asked me to marry him. I thought I had learned my lesson from the last time, and I was determined not to let this dream pass away from me again.

He knew there was a part of me that was off limits, but it was something we agreed not to discuss. He was willing to take me as I was. We talked about settling for second best – but Jude was adamant that he was willing to take whatever I had to give him. So we planned our wedding.

Jude was such a romantic that he wanted to be involved in every minute decision. Our wedding was as much created by him as it was by me.

The night before our wedding, Jude came over to my apartment. He found me sobbing into my pillow. That was such a heartbreaking night for us.

I felt that I was giving up a dream I always kept hidden deep in my heart. I was marrying Jude out of fear that if I didn't, I would never find love again and always be alone, single. Fear that I would lose everything.

Jude was so gentle with me, so caring and loving. But I guess it finally dawned on him that what we had wasn't enough. There was more out there, and we were missing it.

When he ended up walking into the chamber in the church where I was waiting, I knew that it was over. He had a desperate gleam in his eyes. All he asked of me was to be honest with him.

He asked me one question.

I think he already knew the answer even before he asked it.

"Will you ever be able to give me your whole heart?"

That had to have been the hardest question I have ever had to answer. I couldn't lie to him, he deserved more than that. But I knew my answer would break his heart.

"I really don't know."

I owed him honesty, but I prayed it would be enough. I was desperate to give him my whole heart. But a deep part of me knew; I just knew that I would never ever be able to say yes.

With a sigh of resignation, Jude reached for both of my hands and pulled me into a hug. There was a note of finality in that embrace.

With a kiss on the top of my head and a touch of caress on my face, Jude whispered the words I will never forget.

"I can never be second best. I love you. But not enough to settle for only half your heart."

With that, he let me go and walked away. He left by the back door, and in the background, I heard his car drive away.

I stood there in stunned silence. Tears escaping from my eyes. I remember hearing the sound of a broken heart being torn from my throat before I collapsed.

That was how I was found.

Heather and Tracey came around me and hugged me. My father walked in, took one look at me, and then after a glance out the window, he left the room. My mother walked in and started to cry, demanding to know what had happened.

Heather and Tracey gently escorted me out of the room, through the very door that Jude had left through, and into the van that had brought me to the church.

I later found out that my dad announced that there would be no wedding. Both my parents and Jude's parents arranged to send all the catered food to the local women's shelter and to the youth drop-in center.

Everyone wanted to know what had happened.

They blamed Jude for walking out on me and breaking my heart. After days of walking in a daze, I felt strong enough to confess to Heather and Tracey what had really occurred.

One week after that fateful day, Jude called me to see if I was okay. He apologized for leaving me to clear up all the mess. We both agreed that it would be best not to say anything to anyone, other than that it was a mutual decision of both parties not to get married.

I doubt that that was enough to stop all the gossip and speculation, but at that point, I didn't care.

I hadn't seen him in three years, not since that day that he walked out of the church. I'd wondered deep down what would happen if he ever did come back. Now I knew. It wasn't that I still loved him, or that I wanted him back.

"I don't know, Wynne," replied Tracey as she just let me cry and bare my heart. "Scripture tells us that God grants us the desires of our heart. I don't want to spiritualize what you are feeling, hon, but when was the last time you really surrendered your desires to God's will?" Tracey said.

"Surrender? How many times do I need to surrender, Tracey? Sometimes it feels like that is all I do. When am I allowed to say enough is enough, and ask when is it my turn for some happiness? I'm the only single one left in our group. Do you know what it's like to go to bed lonely every night? To not have that special someone there to talk to? Marriage and children are my heart's desires. How can that not be God's will?" I asked.

Deep in my heart, I already knew the answers. But it was nice to vocalize my feelings for once.

"Marriage is hard work. You want to make sure you're

married to someone who can go through those hard times with you," replied Tracey with a bit of a far-off look in her eyes.

"Wynne, I know you are a strong person. Instead of settling for second best, you waited. Sometimes I wish ... well, let's just say not everyone has the strength to do that. When Mr. Right does come along, you'll be able to offer so much more to your marriage, than if you had just jumped the boat and married the first guy who came along." She sighed and rested a hand on my arm.

"You know, sometimes I envy you," she says, her voice small. "You have been able to do things with your life that I can't do because I have a family now. You quit your boring, routine job, you took a huge step by opening your own store, and it's a success. You bought this home and made it into your dream home." Tracey let go of my arm, climbed to her feet, and paced across the room.

"You are able to focus your love and attention on your walk with God, and not worry about a lot of little distractions. Don't beat yourself up because you're still single. Enjoy it while you can," Tracey said. She sank back down into the chair. A dejected look filled her face.

"Sometimes I wish I were still single."

Those little words just about broke my heart. I leaned over and gathered her in my arms. It was my turn now to give her the shoulder she needed and let her cry.

"You don't regret marrying Mike, do you?" I wasn't sure I wanted to hear the answer.

She leaned back and took a deep breath. "Sometimes," Tracey whispered. "Is that so horrible of me?"

How was I to answer this? Part of me was shouting - yes, of course, it's horrible of you. Don't you realize the gift you have? But instead, I just gave her a small smile.

"I knew something was wrong but didn't realize it was this bad. Tracey, I'm so sorry. Are you guys just hitting a bump in the road, maybe?" Who was I to really talk though, right?

"A bump? More like a series of bumps. They just keep getting bigger and bigger. I know there has to be an end in sight, but I don't see a promising one any time soon. The only end I see leads to a lot of hurt and pain."

"Oh, honey," I replied. "I'm so sorry. Have you been able to talk to anyone about this? Are you guys going to be okay?" I asked. I honestly didn't know what to say to her. I didn't want to imagine that things were as bad as she was making it sound, yet I didn't want to trivialize her feelings either.

"Right now, Wynne, I honestly can't say. We'll get through. We always do," Tracey answered with a shake of her head.

"Now, enough about me. It's late, and I do need to get home. But … I am going to find time to get away tomorrow, and I'll drag Heather with me. We'll come for coffee and brainstorm about this party you are so determined to throw. I still don't know why you offered to do this – but since you won't back down, you're going to need all the support you can get."

I walked her to the front door and gave her a big hug. We both needed it. Walking to my bedroom, suddenly feeling rather lonely, I made a decision.

I was going to get a cat.

CHAPTER ELEVEN

kittens cure all

I got my cat, well, kitten.

To be honest, I was the proud owner of two kittens.

I was a sucker for punishment, but I couldn't just take one and leave the other behind. After calling the local animal shelter before I headed into the store, I found out that they had just received two kittens earlier that month.

Today was the first day that they were offering them for adoption.

The animal shelter found these kitties tied up in a bag, and they desperately needed some love and care. When I first saw them, my heart just broke. They looked so sad, lying beside each other. As I was watching, one kitten began to play with the other. I think they were trying to put on a show for me. After hearing how they were found, I just couldn't leave one behind.

In the shelter, they seemed too tame. That was my first mistake - making an assumption.

I was able to place them both in one carrier, complete with a soft blanket for them to lie on. Since they seemed so well-behaved, I decided to take them into the store with me.

That was my second mistake.

I figured I could just leave them in the carrier in my office while I had to work out front. The worker at the shelter told me that with them being young and uncared for, I might find that all they do is sleep for the first day or so. Let me tell you – was she ever wrong.

When I walked into the store, Heather was waiting for me. It was her morning to open, which left me time to get any little running around that I needed to get done. When she saw the carrier, she immediately came over and peered inside to see what I had.

"Kittens. Oh, aren't they adorable? You never told me you were getting kittens. Awww, look at them. Oh, can I hold them? Pretty please?" Heather bent down and opened the carrier door.

"Isn't she just the sweetest thing? Oh, look at her cute little tongue, and tiny nose, and she's so soft. What's your name sweetie pie? Hmmm, little cupcake, what does ole Wynnie here call you?" Heather cooed at the kitten she was holding in her arms. I placed the carrier down and gathered the other kitten into my arms. I decided to let the 'ole Wynnie' comment pass for now.

"I think I'll call this one Jewel, and the one you have … Hmmm, I'm not sure yet," I said to her as I was stroking the fur on this kitten.

She was gorgeous with a black and gold color tone throughout her fur. Right around her collar she had a ring of almost gold … reminding me of a necklace. I think Jewel would fit her perfectly.

"Cocoa. You should name her Cocoa. Look at her coloring … almost like a chocolate brown, the color of frosting on a cake. So soft and sweet." She held the kitten up to her cheek and rubbed the fur across her face.

Cocoa was an excellent name for her, and in all honesty, how could I not have a cat named Cocoa?

Cocoa licked Heather's face, which caused giggles to erupt from Heather. I took it she was a bit ticklish. After a few more cuddles with the kitten in her hand, Heather placed Cocoa back into the carrier and then reached for Jewel to hold as well. After the same routine, holding, cuddling, face tickling giggles, Heather was ready to get back to work. I took the kittens and their carrier into my office in the back and gently told them to go to sleep.

I walked out to the front to grab a cup of coffee, when Heather barricaded me into the corner of the store, behind the counter.

"Wynne Taylor, we need to talk about this party your planning?"Why didn't you call me last night? I would have come over, you know. Whatever possessed him to come over to your home unannounced and just dump on you with this news? He has no right to do that." Heather stood in front of me with her hands on her hips, clearly annoyed with me.

I had to laugh at her a little bit. I'd had all night and morning to process news she'd just recently found out.

"Don't you dare laugh at me, missy. I'm not the one making nonsense-type decisions here. Seriously." Heather rolled her eyes.

I took it she wasn't all that happy with me.

I wasn't all that happy with myself either. But it wasn't like I could back out now. I made a rash emotional decision, and now I needed help to deal with this mess.

"Okay, okay ... I admit I made the decision based on sheer emotion, and yes, I should have called you ... but ... you still love me. Now, let me grab my coffee, and then you can help me get out of this big mess," I admitted while gently nudging her out of my way.

With the way things were looking right then ... I was definitely going to need that coffee.

As I moved away from the door, I heard some gentle noise coming from my office. Ahh, the sounds of two kittens meowing. I smiled softly as I headed to the coffee counter.

I couldn't wait to take them home. I would need to make a list of things to purchase, thank goodness the Dollar Store was nearby. I could grab some cat toys there, as well as some collars and dishes for food and water. Maybe I'd get them their own beds or maybe one big bed for them to sleep in. I didn't want them to get in the habit of sleeping with me in my bed.

Armed with coffee and some little treats, I headed to the

corner table where Tracey and Heather were huddled together with their heads joined, deep in conversation.

"I come bearing gifts," I stated with a bow.

"You've come to try to sweeten us up, more like it," said Heather. She knows me so well.

"Will it help?" I asked sweetly. I made sure I gave my sweet little innocent smile, while I batted my eyelashes at the two.

"If it's chocolate, who cares?" Tracey said as she grabbed the plate of goodies out of my hand.

"So," Tracey stopped to take a bite out of a chocolate macaroon the size of a small child's hand. "Heather and I have decided that this needs to be a spectacular party, one that will take everyone's mind off the fact it's you throwing it. In fact, we'll spread it around that it's the group of us doing it, as old friends of Jude. We'll take the focus completely off of you as the hostess." She popped the rest of the macaroon into her mouth.

"You think that will work?" I said. Somehow I doubted it.

"No, I don't think it will work, but at least we're trying," Heather retorted. I thought I might have insulted her by being skeptical.

"I do appreciate it. What would I do without you two to help me fix my messes? You know I love you … enough to share my chocolate with you, and that's a big deal."

All right, all right, that was a bit cheeky of a reply, but I needed to get back into the good graces of Heather, and I figured a bit of teasing might help.

I glanced at Heather to see if it was working and found her watching me with a thoughtful gleam in her eye.

"What?"

"Have you had any more of your mystery man dreams?"

"Why?" I said. I didn't like the sound of this, nope, not at all.

"What does that have to do with throwing this engagement party?" Tracey asked Heather.

"It doesn't really have anything to do with the party per se, but I'm wondering if she offered to throw this party with a bit of desperation," she answered, still with that thoughtful look in her eye.

"I don't understand," replied Tracey. "How would desperation make her do this?"

"Well, the more she has these dreams, the more frustrated I've noticed her become. I think that instead of being ready to deal with these issues, she just blurted out that she would throw this party. Now there is something else in her life for her to focus on rather than the real heart issues," Heather explained.

"Whoa, hold on a minute, guys. I'm sitting right here." I said with just a bit of frustration in my voice. I don't like being ignored. Nor do I like the fact that Heather was hitting awfully close to home right then.

"Only if you'll admit that I'm right," Heather answered back.

"Why do I have to admit that? So you can psychoanalyze me even more? No. Let's just drop this subject and deal with the issue at hand. Please?" I asked, addressing this question to both gals.

"Well, there's no reason to get your jammies all in a knot." Tracey shot back at me. "Besides, you haven't answered the original question."

"What question?" I asked. "The one about whether or not I've had more dreams." I wasn't really sure I liked how this conversation was going right then.

"Yes, that question," Heather replied with a sigh.

I took my cup of coffee in both hands and brought it to my face. I inhaled slowly, absorbing the aroma within my senses. I took a couple of sips, trying to waste time before having to answer. Fortified, I finally answered.

"Yes, I had a dream last night. We were sitting by a pond. There was a pink blanket on the grass, and he had a beautiful hatbox sitting in his hands. It was gold with a pink ribbon. He was handing me the box, but I was hesitant to take it. I felt a bit afraid, but I took it in my hands and slowly began to undo the ribbon. I didn't open the box, though. I think if I had, all the mysteries of my dreams would be answered, and I wasn't ready for that." I twirled my coffee cup in my hand while I described to them my dream from last night.

"Wouldn't you like to know who he is?" asked Tracey.

"Why? Heather already thinks I know who he is, but I'm just not willing to admit it." I answered her back.

"True," Heather answered. "Have you thought any more about trying to find him?"

"Trying to find whom? Okay, guys, I'm a bit lost here." Tracey butted in before I had a chance to answer.

"Heather seems to think that I'm dreaming of Rich. I think she's wrong. Heather's convinced that if I only try to find Rich and get in touch with him, that might solve all my problems. But I think he's married. So if I do try to get in touch with him, I'll probably end up talking with his wife, and then how do I explain?" was my answer to Tracey. Evidently, I hadn't kept her abreast of this.

"And what if you find out that you're wrong? What then, Wynne?" Heather asked me. "What if he's been single all along, and it's just your stubbornness that has been keeping you apart? What will it hurt?" she asked me.

"It could hurt my heart. That's not a risk I'm willing to take, Heather," I answered.

"TIME OUT," Tracey yelled. Heather and I glanced at her and found her leaning on the table, looking at us rather sternly.

"Yes'm," I said meekly while kicking Heather under the table.

"All right. I can tell this is a somewhat sticky topic between the two of you, and it's obviously not going to be dealt with today. So can we please deal with the topic on hand … we have a party to plan." Tracey lectured us in her 'don't give me any nonsense' mom tone.

While she was forcing us to calm down, I heard a slight commotion in the background. I glanced at Lily to see if she knew what was going on, but she was looking at me with a worried look on her face. She gestured toward my office. What could possibly have been making that noise? The kittens were in their crate, and besides, I was told all they would do was sleep today. What could they possibly have done?

I quickly got up and started to walk towards my office. That's when the noise grew and intensified. Glass shattered. The kittens meowed. I freaked.

"Did you lock the crate gate?" Heather asked me as she followed me to the door.

"I think so," I replied as I opened the door cautiously. I peered around the door, amazed at what I saw.

As I stood there in shock, one of the kittens darted out. Before I could react, it was past me. The other one almost made it as well, but Heather grabbed a hold of it as it whizzed by.

Behind me, I heard Tracey and Lily calling for the kitten. I had no idea where it had gone, but I would let them deal with it for the moment. Right then, I had to face the mess in my office.

The sight that greeted me as I opened the door was definitely one that will stay in my memory forever. If I had time to scrapbook, that was a sight that I would have taken a picture of. I had a thought in my head for a label, but it wasn't one that should be spoken out loud.

The glass sound that I heard was my lamp being knocked over and crashing to the ground. Any papers that were on my desk had mysteriously ended up all over my floor. My seat cushion was in shreds. My bottle of water was all over my desk; obviously, I had forgotten to snap on the lid when I last used it. The dish of little candies that I liked to keep on my desk was scattered about, the dish was on the floor unbroken, but the candies were everywhere.

Ribbon that had been originally rolled up is now unrolled, and I wasn't sure if the little puddles of water on my floor were actually water or something else unmentionable. What had happened to my sweet little kittens that were supposed to sleep all day?

Heather glanced around me and began to giggle. I turned to look at her and gave her one of those 'you've got to be kidding me' types of looks. She just kept on giggling.

It was hard to stay stern when she giggled. I tried to keep it in, but it was so hard to do, so eventually, I found myself joining in. There's nothing like two girls giggling to attract attention. Up walked Tracey, holding the other kitten in her arms. She peeked inside the office, gasped, and then the tell-tale signs of a smile also began to show on her face.

Soon all three of us were giggling. I left Heather and Tracey holding the offending criminals while I walked inside to search for evidence of the crate being left unlocked. Amazingly I found it unlatched. I glared at Heather accusingly, but she just shrugged her shoulders, unable to speak due to her giggling. Tracey then winked at me and pointed.

I was standing in a wet puddle. I groaned. They giggled even harder. The kittens were wiggling in their captors' hands, trying to get free. I grabbed each offender and placed them in the crate, making sure I locked it soundly this time. They made sure their outrage in little meows was heard, but at that point, I was deaf to their cries.

My sanctuary had been destroyed, and my designer shoe was wet with what, I really didn't want to guess at, and my friends were just standing there giggling. This was now officially a crisis. I definitely needed more coffee and chocolate.

With my office cleaned up and the supposedly 'angelic' kittens finally sleeping, I found myself back at the table trying to make plans for the engagement party I mistakenly offered to throw. Armed with enough chocolate to satisfy any pre-menopausal woman, we got down to business.

We finally came to the conclusion that we would hold the party in our church basement. Tracey loved to make homemade cards, so she would create invitations to the party. Heather would create her delicious masterpieces – desserts only, and I would be in charge of the decorating.

Now, this would be fun. I would have to find out what type of things Stacey liked so I could turn the versatile basement of the church into a beautiful room.

In my head, I had visions of pink lace, tulle, and ribbon all over the place. Not a pretty vision. I hoped she would like soft colors, but not too girly. After all, this would not be just for the bride-to-be.

Perhaps some heavy cream-colored tablecloths with classic dark napkins. For the centerpieces, we could fill assorted vases with water and clear cellophane wrapping paper, and sprinkle some pink sparkles throughout the water. I'd place a floater candle on top of the vases and add some tea light candles around each vase. Not too girly, or masculine. Simple but elegant. Oh, and some Gerbera flowers all over the room as well. Since it was winter, I might have to buy fake ones, but if they were nice enough, no one would mind.

As thoughts raced through my head, I caught a glimmer of what I would like my own engagement party to look like. I allowed the thought that I was doing this more for me than for Stacey and Jude to linger for just a second before I tossed it out and stubbornly announced to myself that it had nothing to do with me personally.

Ignoring the obvious, I took a walk through my store, dusting this, touching that, and doing anything I could to take my mind off my reasoning for offering to host the party.

Things were a bit slow that day in the store, so while Lily closed up, I'd take my kittens home and introduce them to their new place. I heard them meowing in my office, they were probably ready to get out of their carrier and run free.

If this afternoon was any indication as to what my life as a new pet owner would be like, I didn't think I'd have a quiet evening for a while.

What was I ever thinking when I decided to get both kittens, I had no idea.

CHAPTER TWELVE

when mother calls

After an evening of de-cluttering and kitty-proofing my home, I spent some quiet time going through some old bridal magazines trying to get ideas of what we could do for Jude and Stacey's party.

I used to hide my magazines from any guests that came through my door, until I realized that it was quite normal for single women to have any number of bridal magazines scattered throughout their homes, with sticky notes protruding out of various pages within the magazine. After all, let's be honest. No matter our age, wedding-filled dreams are a part of who we are.

Every woman knew exactly what she wanted her wedding dress to look like, she'd already picked out the music, the song she would walk down the aisle to, and who would be in the wedding party.

For some, the invitations were chosen; she just waited for the groom's name to appear on them. Some might call them fantasy dreams, but for those of us who lived this fantasy life, it was our dream that our plans would one day become reality.

While I was read '21 Ways to Fool-Proof Your Wedding', and 'How to Create the Wedding of Your Dreams, Not Your Mothers', my phone rang.

I jumped, startled, which scared the sleeping kittens beside me.

In the midst of trying to reach the phone, while not losing my page and trying not to get scratched by the frightened kittens, I managed to spill the hot coffee that I had balanced on the edge of my armrest.

I answered the phone with a "hot hot hot – ouch," before I heard my mother's voice shouting through the line.

"Wynne, are you okay? What happened? Is this a bad time?"

"No, no, it's a fine time," I answered while skipping around the floor, untangling myself from the afghan I had somehow gotten caught up in.

While trying to avoid the ever-growing puddle of coffee that surrounded my feet, I noticed out of the corner of my eye the kittens running through the doorway, heading to who knows where. They would be fine, right? Not get into anything, right?

My lips to God's ears.

"Well, you don't sound fine. What happened this time?" Mom asked with a hint of disbelief in her voice.

"What do you mean by 'this time'? It's not like things happen to me a lot, Mom. I just spilled some coffee on myself while trying to reach the phone," I answered in annoyance. The way my mom talks, you would think I was a walking klutz.

"Wynne, don't take that tone with me. The last time I talked with you, you'd twisted your ankle while wearing your new dress shoes. Or what about the time you got that huge bump on your forehead by walking into a post while talking on your cell phone? Sometimes I think your head is up in 'la-la land,'" she exclaimed while listing all my most recent mishaps.

"All right, already. How are you doing, Mom?" I asked.

"I'm fine. I'm calling to ask if you're feeling okay?" she asked me.

"I'm feeling fine, Mom. Why? What's up?"

"What do you mean what's up? I just received a call from Jude's mother. That's what's up. She wanted to let me know what a nice daughter I have. How sweet and how kind it is of you to throw Jude and his fiancée an engagement party."

The silence between us was palpable.

"An engagement party, Wynne. Do you know how stupefied I felt? I had no idea that he was engaged, let alone that you, of all people, would throw him a party to celebrate it. What made you do that, and why didn't you tell me?" It's amazing how mothers can sound both exasperated and astonished at the same time. It must be a gift they acquire.

"I just found out as well that he was engaged, and I was so shocked that I just blurted it out. I couldn't very well take it back. Besides, I'm actually looking forward to doing it now. You know how much I love to throw parties. Tracey and Heather are helping me, and we're making a joint effort, so that it won't appear that I'm the one throwing it," I tried to explain to her.

My mom had a tendency to enjoy being in the middle of all the fluff when something big was going on.

"Well, of course, it will appear you are the one throwing it. Do you think no one will know? Nancy is practically bragging about it. As far as she is concerned, it's only right that the girl who broke her son's heart throw this party. Don't you care how this will look? Everyone will feel sorry for you … the girl who got left behind," Mom explained with a tone of pity in her voice.

Something told me that this wasn't a short conversation.

"Now, I've been thinking," Oh-oh. Definitely not a good sign when I hear this coming from her lips. "What we need to do is get you a date for this party. That way, no one will think you're still brokenhearted over losing Jude. It'll show that you have moved on with your life," she said proudly.

"And where do you propose I find this mystery man, oh mother dearest?" I asked a bit sarcastically. As if I could just create a man from my dreams, make him pop out of nowhere. We lived in a small town. You would think that if there were any available men in this town, I would have noticed them already.

"Well," she said a bit hesitantly, "how about you just leave that up to me?"

I laughed.

"Seriously. You concentrate on the party, and I'll find a date for you. No, no, don't worry - I already have the perfect gentleman in mind. He's handsome, Christian, and very sensitive. He'll be just perfect for you. I think it's a wonderful idea."

I couldn't stop laughing. Sensitive? What does she take me for?

What could it hurt? I'd already done enough damage to my image as far as my friends were concerned. So, what harm would bringing a blind date to an engagement party be? If it was so obvious that I was the one who was throwing this party, then it would be just as obvious that I was desperate enough to need to bring a blind date to it.

"Sure, Mom. You go ahead. Just make sure he's nice, okay, and that he knows this is for one night only. Nothing else, okay, Mom? Promise?" I replied.

"Really. You'll let me bring someone? Sure honey, no promises. Gotcha. Okay. Well, you have a good night now, and I'll talk to you later."

She probably wanted to end this conversation before I had the chance to change my mind. I didn't blame her. Smart move on her part.

So why did I have a feeling I was going to regret letting her play matchmaker?

CHAPTER THIRTEEN

let this be a dream

I was happy.

My feet were wet, and my jeans were sticking to my legs, but I felt happy. I could hear the waves, the soft gentle sound ringing in my ears. The sun was setting, vibrant shades of orange and red.

What's that saying? 'Red in the morning, sailor's warning; red at night, sailor's delight.' I felt at peace, all was right in my world.

I glanced down and realized that there was a pair of arms surrounding my waist, holding tightly onto me. I leaned my head to the side, and warm lips settled against my skin. I leaned back and felt … loved. I was happy, at peace, and it was a wonderful feeling.

I faced the lake, with the waves gently crashing onto my feet, and there were sailboats in the distance, bobbing up and down, in tune with the rise and fall of the waves.

I imagined myself on that boat. How peaceful that would be.

With that one thought, I found myself on that very boat. My feet were no longer wet. In fact, I had designer sandals on with a summer dress swirling around my ankles. There was a gentle breeze that was lifting my hair off my neck and gently caressing me, it kind of tickled.

I looked around, and all I saw was water. It was even more peaceful than I thought. I heard footsteps walk across the deck, felt arms come around me, and saw wine glasses in each hand. I took one, brought it to my nose, and smelled it. It was a sweet smell, like apple juice. I took a sip, letting the sensation of the sweet and bitter taste fill my mouth. I leaned my head back, and heard a voice whisper in my ear. "I love you."

Tingly sensations began to sweep over me in waves. The three most romantic words that my soul had longed to hear. I closed my eyes and held those words deep in my heart.

I love you, I love you, I love you.

I could hear that deep voice huskily repeating those words to me. A soft whisper in my ear, spoken with hidden promises of lasting love, honor, and commitment. An eternal love. An eternal promise.

I rolled my head to the side. I wanted to turn around, to whisper those secrets that are hidden deep within my very being. I felt the soft caress of the wind against my neck. It began to tickle. I brought my hand up to rub that very spot when I felt my finger being bitten. Bitten? Ouch – that hurt.

I quickly rose from my slouched position on the couch and held my finger. There were little tiny bite marks. That wasn't the wind caressing my neck; it was a little kitten licking me. I put my hand to my neck, and it was wet. Those weren't gentle kisses from my dream man. They were little kitten kisses.

So much for my romantic dream.

I scooped up the kitten responsible for waking me from my dream and cuddled it against my cheek. If I closed my eyes, I could almost hear that soft soothing sound of the waves while they washed upon the sand. I could almost feel those warm arms holding me close, and I could almost recapture that feeling of timeless love. Almost.

Who was this mystery man? Could it be Rich, as Heather believed? What if it was him? Why couldn't I let this go, why did I continually hold onto that dream in my heart of my first love?

Grow up Wynne. Time to move on. What would it hurt, though, to perhaps do a quick little search as Heather kept encouraging me to do? Unless he was important or something, I doubted very much I would find anything on him.

No one would need to know. If I didn't find anything, then I could tell Heather, and that would be the end of it all. And if I did find something? Well, I doubted that would happen.

I glanced at the clock. It was only a little after ten at night. Just enough time to do a quick search, check my email and head off to bed. I could have used another cup of coffee, but since I was fresh out of decaf, I'd have to enjoy a nice cup of hot chocolate.

While the kettle was going, I routed through my fridge to see if I had any whip cream left over. There's nothing like a cup of hot chocolate with whip cream on top. Well, if it has chocolate shavings, it might be a little bit better, but it was late, and I was all out.

Mental note to self: make a fresh batch of shavings tomorrow.

Armed with a large cup of hot chocolate, I settled back on my couch, moved the kittens to the other side, and placed my laptop on my knees. I made sure my hot chocolate is safely sitting on my side table, and that the kittens were safely on the other side of the couch before I logged on. I bypassed my email for the moment, since, after all, this quest wouldn't take much time, and if I got this out of the way, then it would be off my mind.

Where to start? I brought up Google's home page and entered 'Rich Carradine'. Amazingly, it turned out that there were over 70,000 different sites that have both the word Rich and Carradine in them. Like I was going to search them all. Taking a quick glance at the first few pages was like taking a quick dip in a fantasy novel – instant and utter confusion. There had to be an easier way to find information here. So I decided to type in the name of the university I last heard he taught at. Just as I was about to hit Search, the phone rang.

Heather's perky voice was on the other line.

"Hey girly, it's not too late to call, is it?" she asked with a slight laugh to her tone.

"No. It's still early, and only the bored and married are in bed. What's up?" I responded with a bit of sarcasm. I heard more muffled giggling from her, and I felt a bit annoyed.

"Sorry," she answered back, still laughing. "I had a little bit too much chocolate and coffee tonight, and Matt wants to go to bed, so he suggested I bug you instead of him," she explained among her many giggling episodes.

One thing I learned about Heather right from the start is that she is very sensitive to caffeine. Too much in her system, and she is bouncing off the walls. It's a scary sight, actually.

"Nice guy you have there. He married you, so why do I get stuck with you whenever he doesn't want to deal with you?" I made sure I laughed a little when I said it – did I mention that she is very sensitive emotionally when she's had too much caffeine as well?

"Because he knows how much you love me, and you're the only one besides him who will put up with me. Those were his exact words too."

"So, what are you doing anyway?"

I hesitated a little bit. Should I really tell her what I was doing? I could only imagine her response.

"Hmmm, I'm on the net. Nothing too important. Just doing a little searching, wasting mindless brain cells searching for anything and everything that comes into my head. So ... what about you? What did you do this evening that caused you to over-load on caffeine?" I asked, hoping to change the subject.

"The chocolate and coffee, you mean? Oh, Tracey stopped by to chat. I was in the middle of trying out a new recipe, so of course, we had to taste-test it, and nothing goes better with choco-late than coffee. I think between the two of us, we both drank a full pot. I should have made decaf."

I chuckled.

"And before you ask why I didn't call you, I tried but your phone was busy. Then one thing led to another, and Tracey just left a few moments ago. Don't worry, I saved you some of my experiments. It's quite good, actually. If Matt could keep his hands off them, I'll bring some into the store tomorrow," Heather promised.

"Hmmm, it must be good if Matt likes it. What did you make? If it's chocolate, you know I'll like it," I said to her. It wasn't fair of her to dangle a little piece of chocolate in front of my face and not tell me what she made.

"Oh, you'll like it, all right. But you'll have to wait and see. It's a bit hard to explain. So … what were you searching for when I called? Something for your kittens, furniture for your home, a new recipe, or maybe you took my advice and started to look for Rich?" she asked. She's like a hound dog that catches a faint snip of a rabbit. She'll go rooting in every little hole, until she finds what she's searching for.

I stayed silent for a moment. I didn't want to lie to her. But I wasn't quite ready to admit that I gave in either.

"You did, didn't you? You did a search for Rich. I knew you would. So, what did you find? Come on, girl – don't get all quiet on me now," she exclaimed, with an eager tone to her voice.

I could just picture a wide smile on her face, and that '*I knew it*' gleam in her eye. If she wasn't sitting down, she was probably doing a little jig on her floor, and if she was sitting down, she most likely had one of her arms raised in victory.

"All right, All right." I sighed in resignation.

"Yes, I did a quick search, just to satisfy you. Are you happy now?"

"Happy? Of course, I'm happy. Have you found anything? Have you looked in the right places?" Heather asked. "Did you search his name? The school where he teaches? Did you try to find his phone number? Did you look very hard, or hardly looked?" She was like a dog searching for his lost bone. Should I tell her?

"No, Heather. I just did a quick search of his name. Just before you called, I thought of typing in the school's website, but do you know something I don't know? You seem to have a lot of suggestions. Maybe you've already done all the hard work – do you want to fill me in?" I asked her with a hint of accusation in my voice. I was starting to get annoyed, and I was really not sure why.

"You know what? I'm starting to not like your tone right now. I think it's time I let you go. It's probably time I should go and head to bed anyway. Oh, I forgot to tell you. Your Latte Ladies' group is meeting in the morning for an emergency meeting. I'll see you in the morning, okay?" With that being said, Heather hung up the phone.

Great. Now I'd done it. She was probably just trying to offer suggestions, and here I went and bit her head off. Jesus, please forgive me. I'd apologize to her in the morning, and I promised not to be upset if she didn't bring me any of the treats that she'd made tonight.

With those thoughts in mind, I found myself typing in the various suggestions that she'd made in searching for Rich. I typed in the name of the school I last knew him to teach at. As I waited for the web page to load up, I began to feel a little queasy in my stomach. I clicked on the link to the Alumni page.

As I scrolled down, I really found myself a bit nervous. What if I saw his picture and description? Did I want to read it? What if he was married, how would I react? What if he was single? Was it right if I prayed that he was still single, or should I pray that he was married? What would I do if I found out he was still single? It wasn't like I could just call him up out of the blue and say, 'hey, I've been dreaming of you lately, and I think I'm still in love with you'. Could I really say that? I shook my head – of course, I couldn't. Who in their right mind would start off a conversation like that?

Just before I decided I'm the world's biggest chicken ever and clicked off the site, I saw his name. It jumped out at me. I took a deep breath and closed my eyes. I was either too much of a chicken or I needed some added strength. Unsure which, I said a quick 'God help me' prayer and opened my eyes.

There he was. As handsome as ever. With the same wavy hair,

sparkling eyes, he looked the same, only a bit older. My stomach did one of those little fluttery dances, and my heart beat just a little bit faster.

Glancing through his bio beside his picture, I noticed it said nothing about his family. That could be a good thing, right? I quickly glanced up to see if any other bios contained personal information and saw several where they talked about the wives and children. Whew. So, maybe he still was single.

I felt a huge smile creep over my face, and I giggled. Me. Giggling. It was almost like some hope for the future had re-entered my heart. I wasn't sure what I will do with this, though.

It took me a few moments to realize I really didn't need to do any further searches, so I shut down my computer, held this new thought close to my heart, and headed off to bed. Who knew, maybe my dreams would be different tonight.

CHAPTER FOURTEEN

latte ladies

I was late.

The last time I was late for one of my Latte Ladies' meetings, the goodies had disappeared, and I was volunteered to work a craft table at the local Kids' Fair day. I didn't mind working at the Kids' Fair, but the fact they didn't leave me any goodies really hurt.

There they all were, sitting at the corner table. I could see a basket in the middle. Must be Heather's treat that she made last night. Please don't let it be empty.

"Good morning," Lily greeted me from the counter as I stopped to pour myself a cup of coffee.

"Hi there, Miss Lily. How are you doing this morning? I thought Heather was coming in to open up." I looked around to see if I could spot Heather.

"Oh, Heather did. But I knew you had your Latte Ladies this morning, so I thought I would come in just in case it was a bit busy. With this being the busy Christmas season, I just figured you deserved to sit down and enjoy your coffee rather than popping up here to help out with customers," Lily replied with a cheeky smile.

Okay, okay. I admit it. I'm a hands-on type of person, and I can't seem to sit still when the store is full of customers. If I'm not at the front counter ringing in their purchases, then I'm browsing throughout the store, chatting with those who come in, offering suggestions, and pouring coffee.

After quickly sticking my tongue out at Lily for her comment, I grabbed my coffee, fresh muffin, and headed over to the table.

"All right, where's the chocolate?"

"You snooze, you lose. You should know that by now," said Joan as she quickly placed her hand in the basket to grab one of those delicious treats.

"Awww, be nice, Joan. Wynne looks like she had a bit of a rough morning. Look, she's even wearing her shirt inside out. I think she deserves one of those goodies," Judy replied, as she gently patted my arm in sympathy.

I quickly glanced down at my top and realized she was right. It was inside out.

"I didn't sleep well," I muttered quietly as I left the table feeling a bit flustered and entered the washroom to change my shirt around. I couldn't believe I walked out the front door like this.

As I walked out the bathroom door, I heard laughter coming from the table. Hoping that laughter wasn't directed at me, I peeked around the corner to see what was going on. Judy was leaning into the table with an intense look on her face. That could only mean one thing. She was telling one of her stories.

Judy McNeil is the mother of our group. I think of her as 'old and wise' although she really isn't all that old. Judy has a whole passel of children, a total of six if I counted right last time. I'm not sure how she does it, to be honest, yet she never seems to be worn out. If Judy isn't at home with her family, you'll find her bringing some home-baked goodies to a lady in our church, volunteering at one of the many functions that always seem to be happening in our town, or joining us for our Latte Ladies.

I remember her saying once that Latte Ladies was an outlet for her, a venue that God used to revitalize and bring some joy into her life. That caused me to really think about what Latte Ladies meant to me.

It used to just be a bible study that I went to once a week, until it was this very group of ladies that stood by me when my life seemed to be in shambles. Now, I thank God for them on a daily basis. He used them to touch my life in so many different ways.

"Now that looks better," piped up a cheeky Joan as I sat down in my chair. "You must have had a rough night to not remember how to get dressed. Here, I saved you a treat. You will just love them. She calls them Turtle squares, and they go perfectly with a cup of coffee," chattered Joan, as I reached into the basket, with the hopes that someone at least saved me one treat.

"Thanks. Yes, I had a rough night, and a rough morning, and I definitely need this right now. Nothing takes the blues away like chocolate in the morning." I took a bite of the delicious treat.

"Oh, get ready … here comes her reaction," said Tracey.

"Hmmm, ohhhhh, hmmmm," I moaned as I took a bite of the delicious treat. I was known to savor chocolate. To take a bite of any type of chocolate, whether it's a cookie, square, or even a chocolate bar, and not savor that first sweet taste as it melted in your mouth, was just wrong.

There was a technique to this I have discovered. I'd tried time and time again to explain it to the girls, but they didn't appreciate a good thing when they bit into it.

First, you needed to smell the chocolate. You could always get your taste buds going on hyperdrive just by one smell. Could you smell the mint or caramel in what you were about to enjoy? Maybe it was hazelnut? You'll never know, though, until you smell it first.

Then close your eyes as you take that first bite. Gently sink your teeth into the soft chocolate, let it sit on your tongue for a few seconds, and savor the unique feeling of that chocolate as it melted.

Allow the sensation to sink in; to settle into your very soul.

First, it was one of those 'ah' moments, and then you get that feeling that all was right with the world.

Nothing else existed when you had a piece of chocolate in your mouth.

I always got teased by these ladies for how much I enjoyed my dessert. I'd never hidden the fact that chocolate was one of my passions in life.

I think that was why Chocolate Blessings was so successful. It's a full-blown passion for me. How many people could honestly say that they took their top passion in life and made it a success?

"Make fun of me all you want, Tracey, but, you know that you love chocolate just as much as I do," I said after I enjoyed my first bite.

"True, but no one else has made eating chocolate an art," she came back at me.

"Ladies, ladies … enjoy your chocolate and call it even," Pastor Joy said to us with a smile on her face.

"We might need to give Wynne an extra treat this morning. She's going to need it, I think." Judy patted my arm again.

"I'll take the chocolate, but why do you think I need it?" I asked, curiously.

"Well, dear," Judy began, "we heard about this party that you are throwing, and we are all a bit concerned. Now don't get me wrong. We stand behind you, and we will help you plan it, but we were there for you when he left. We're a bit concerned about how you are handling all this right now."

I looked at the ladies with, what I was sure was coming across as, an exasperated look.

"Tracey put you up to this, didn't she?" I asked. I smiled at them, perhaps trying to reassure them that I really was okay.

"No, hon." Pastor Judy said softly. "Jude's mother, Nancy, called me up yesterday to tell me. She assumed you would want to use the church basement to hold this party, and she wanted to make sure that it would be available," she explained.

I slumped in my chair at this news.

"Nancy called you? Great. I can imagine what she had to say

about this."

"Yes, she had a bit more to say, but that is neither here nor there. Wynne, what I'm concerned about is the fact that you offered to throw this party. You know you don't have to do this. I'm sure one of us, or any other lady in our church for that fact, would have offered to throw this party had we found out. Actually, I think Nancy would have loved to have thrown a huge shower for her son and his fiancée."

"In all honesty, it was a spur-of-the-moment decision. Jude stopped over unannounced and told me the news. I was a bit shocked and overreacted. Tracey came over for our girls' night, and because I had been embarrassed about how I reacted to his news, I just blurted out that I would throw the party," I admitted to the group.

"But, the more I think about it, the better it sounds to me. If I throw this party, then everyone will realize that I'm not pining over my ex-fiancé and that I'm okay with him getting married. Everyone knows how much I love to throw parties, so no one should think twice about this, right?" I asked, sincerely hoping for their agreement.

There was a moment of silence around the table. I started to doubt that I would receive their agreement.

"Wynne, honey. Are you serious?" asked Joan.

"I thought I was," I answered a bit hesitantly. The way the ladies stared at me, a little bit of worry seeped into my mind.

"Wynne, we were there, remember, when you broke down sobbing because he up and left you at the church alone. We've been there when you have been angry with God because you thought He wasn't hearing your heart's cry. We heard you when you told us of your secret hope that if Jude was ever to come back to town, you might get back together with him." A sad smile crossed Judy's face. "You can't fool us, honey, no matter how hard you try."

"I know. But obviously, it is God's will for me to be alone right now. Otherwise, Jude would have come back sooner and without a fiancée in tow. I have to accept that. I have to accept that there is a strong probability I will be single for the rest of my days. I might not like the idea, doesn't mean I have to hide from it, though, right?" I asked her.

Why was everyone committed to making me face my deep issues with this whole Jude/engagement party blow-up?

"Just because Jude obviously isn't the one for you, that doesn't mean God wants you to be single for the rest of your life. Look at me. I didn't get married until I was thirty-five," Pastor Joy admitted. "God has just been preparing you, getting you ready so that when that perfect man does come along, there will be nothing holding you back."

I knew she was trying to encourage me, but for a pep talk - it sucked.

"Don't you think that throwing this party, shows that I have moved on with my life? I really don't think this was such a bad idea. It's just one friend throwing another friend an engagement party. What's so wrong with that?" I asked them with a hint of desperation in my voice.

Tracey handed me another chocolate turtle and pushed my coffee cup closer to my hands.

"There's nothing wrong with a mere friend throwing another friend a party. But when it's an ex-fiancée throwing the party, then it looks like she is trying really hard to prove, not only to herself but also to the rest of the world, that she has really moved on with her life," Tracey responded.

I took a deep sigh. I never could hide anything from these ladies, and I wasn't about to start trying then. I might as well admit the truth, open myself up completely, and trust that they will still love me enough, in the end, to help me plan this party.

"Fine. I admit that I had some issues and that offering to throw that party probably wasn't the best idea I'd ever had. I will also admit that I probably still have some feelings left for Jude. But, and this is a big but, I don't love him anymore, nor am I jealous that he is getting married and I'm not!" I exclaimed to the group.

They all stared at me with their eyebrows raised. I guess they didn't believe me.

"Okay, okay. So I might be a little bit jealous that he's getting married. But only a little bit. What girl wouldn't be? But I made the choice not to marry him three years ago. If I was still holding some unrealized feelings towards him, I have to let them go. I don't understand why he's getting married, and I'm not. I don't understand why God is withholding that desire from me. It's like He keeps dangling that dream in front of me, and yanking it whenever I start to hope too much on it. That's not fair," I cried out.

I definitely needed more chocolate now. Seeing that the basket was now empty, I rose from my seat and hurried over to the counter to fill a plate full of muffins and cookies. I needed something to take my mind off my emotions; otherwise, I would start crying soon.

There was a nice lull at the table when I returned with the plate of muffins. As everyone helped themselves to the treats, I ventured some quick peeks at all their faces. Some were watching me with speculation in their eyes; others were fixated solely on their muffin or cookie.

I took a deep breath. Perhaps I could steer the conversation away from my unsettled issues and onto the major issue at hand. The party.

"Admitting that there are still some issues that I obviously have to deal with is one thing. But actually having to plan this party is another. I need some help," I asked them.

Joan immediately rushed to my rescue. Bless her heart.

"Well, of course, you need help, sweetie. That's why we are here. I've already made a list of the major tasks that need to be done. You just tell me what you have planned, and we'll go from there."

So with the conversation successfully changing directions, we spent the remaining hour of our study making party plans. Once again, these ladies had saved the day.

CHAPTER FIFTEEN

the ambush

"Hey, girl. Your sign says you're closed, so come with me." I heard a familiar voice call out to me as the door bells jingled their merry tune.

"Heather? What brings you by? You should be at home snuggled up to your hubby in front of your roaring fire." I smiled at her while continuing to close up the store.

"Matt is at a meeting tonight at the church. The men's group is having a 'chef contest' tonight. I made Matt take my apron and hat with him so that he looks like a real chef," she explained to me while she started to giggle.

"Which apron did you give him, Heather?" I asked. "Your professional white one, or the girly pink one that I bought you for Christmas last year?"

"Well, I stuffed it all into a plastic bag, so he won't find out until he gets there – but of course, the pink one." Heather giggled.

I could just see Matt's face when he pulled out his chef's uniform in front of all those guys.

"Too bad you didn't have someone to take a picture," I said to her as I gathered up my coat and purse.

"Oh, but I do. I called Pastor Miles, who is leading the group tonight. I told him what I did, and he can't wait to see Matt all dressed up. He's agreed to take a few pictures for me," she said as she grabbed my arm and led me to the front door.

"Now that's a sight I definitely wouldn't want to miss. So, where are we going?" I asked her as I locked up the door and started out towards her car.

"I thought we could go out for dinner tonight, just you and I. It's been a while since we've gone out and had some girly fun. I'm in the mood for some nice Italian food, how does that sound?" she asked me while doing a little dance in the snow by her car door.

"Well, you definitely seem to be in quite the mood tonight," I said to her. "What's up? I didn't think we were doing the girly night thing until next week?" I asked with a hint of hesitation in my voice.

Heather was normally a spontaneous type of girl, but she was acting a bit, hmm, I don't know, strange tonight. Something was definitely up.

"What do you mean, what's up? Why does something have to be up when all I want to do is go and have some fun girly time tonight? I don't want to wait until next week." She stopped her twirling and stood there with her hands on her hips, almost like she was ready to do battle.

I placed my hands up in the air. "All right, all right. I give up." It felt good to laugh. I needed this tonight.

"Good. Now get in the car and let's go. I'm hungry," Heather said to me with a sigh as she stepped into her car and started it up.

We ended up at Mama Rose's, the best little spot in town for Italian food. I absolutely loved their Fettuccini Alfredo. I usually ordered take-out here at least every week as a special treat to myself. Once in a while, I'd come in and dine, but not too often.

The place had a real romantic feeling to it, and it was too much to handle at times.

The moment we walked in, we were instantly greeted by Mama Rose herself.

"Wynnie, Wynnie. So good to see you," she greeted me while enfolding me in a warm hug and planting kisses on each cheek. "It's been too long since you came in here. I haven't seen you in over a week now. I made a cheesecake just for you, and you never come. Wynnie, Wynnie, what am I gonna do with you?" She patted each cheek gently.

"Heather. Now, this is a treat. So good to see you. I remember when you girls used to come in here all the time. Then you get married, and you don't come in as much. And where is that handsome man of yours?" She glanced behind us.

"It's just us, Mama Rose. We're having a girls' night tonight," I say to her as she takes us to a secluded table.

"A girls' night. Just the thing you needed, I think. Now you come this way. Best spot in the room, a nice corner where you girls can have a quiet evening. And I will have a mochaccino with chocolate whip cream and shavings to you in a jiffy. Come, come." Mama Rose clapped her hands while leading us to our table.

"Mochaccino and cheesecake. Mama Rose, you spoil me." I placed my arm around her thick waist and gave it a squeeze.

"Ah, Wynnie, you need to be spoilt every now and then," she replied as a blush swept across her face.

"Now, sit, chat and enjoy." And with that, she left us and disappeared behind the counter to make our sweet drinks.

As we sat, I glanced around the restaurant. I absolutely love how Mama Rose has created the ambiance for the room. White Christmas lights are wrapped around the walls and create a soft glow throughout the room. Ivy is intertwined amongst the lights, and there are long wooden shelves along each wall holding antique items that range in size and detail.

On one wall, you could find white water pitchers set among antique-looking mirrors that are surrounded by either potted plants or flowers. There were wall sconces everywhere with dimmed lights to help create the soft atmosphere that was part of this place. Soft classical music is being played somewhere.

You almost expected to see musicians suddenly appear, walking among the tables, serenading each couple as they hold hands and gaze into each other's eyes. On each table is a cream-colored tablecloth, complete with a dazzling place setting and a candleholder.

Each corner of the room holds a tall plant, and there are mirrors situated in the perfect spots around the room to help catch the soft glow from the candles, and lights. The perfect setting for romance.

After a server brought our mochaccinos, Heather and I settled in for a girl fest.

I was feeling a bit leery of where our discussions might lead us. You never know with Heather what journey her thoughts will take you on. I figured it might be safer if I was to start the journey before she actually did.

"Okay, Heather, fess up. What do you have up your sleeve?" I asked her. With all her dancing, laughing, and sly looks, I knew something was up.

"Well, why don't we just enjoy our chocolate drink, eat some good food, and then go from there?" Heather suggested while she toyed with the glass in her hand.

"I'm game," I told her. "As long as you promise to spill later on. I'm not going to let you get out of whatever it is you have to say that easily."

Heather just laughed at me as our server came to the table with complimentary garlic bread from Mama Rose. She'd even topped half of it with melted cheese, yum, just the way I liked it.

We both decided to order our usual. I had the fettuccini while Heather ordered the special three-cheese lasagna. If we worked this right, we would sit here long enough to enjoy our food, chat up a storm with each other, and still leave room for dessert at the end. When Mama Rose makes one of her special cheesecakes, you are just not allowed to pass that up. I was really hoping that she made her special Turtles Cheesecake or even a Chocolate Chip Cheesecake.

After chatting about normal girl things, from the likes of the new shoes Heather bought this week, to my need for new throw cushions on my couch (thanks to my new pets), Heather decided to drop a bomb on me.

"So, Wynne. I got a hold of Rich and found out he is still single." Boom.

mama rose's special cheesecake

Whether it be Christmas or birthdays or 'just because it's been awhile', one dessert my family asks for is cheesecake. Specifically Chocolate Chip Cheesecake. I keep trying new flavors, scouring the internet for the 'best' cheesecake recipe out there...but in the end, this is the one they want - and trust me when I say it's ridiculously easy to make. Plus...you don't need a water bath for this one!

MAMA ROSE'S SPECIAL CHEESECAKE

INGREDIENTS:

For the base:

- 1 1/2 cup graham cracker crumbs
- 2 tbsp sugar
- 1 tbsp brown sugar
- 7 tbsp butter (melted)

- 4 pkgs (8 oz each) Philadelphia cream cheese (I've tried other brands and this one is the best to use - softened)
- 1 cup sugar
- 1 cup sour cream
- 1 1/2 tsp vanilla
- 1/8 tsp salt
- 4 eggs (room temperature and lightly beaten)
- 1 bag of mini chocolate chips

STEPS FOR THE BASE:

1. Preheat oven to 325.
2. Prepare crust by combining graham cracker crumbs and sugars and mix well.
3. Add melted butter and use a fork to combine.
4. Press crumbs into a 9" springform pan and press firmly into the bottom and up the sides of your pan.
5. Set aside

STEPS FOR THE CHEESECAKE

- In a large bowl (or stand mixer) add cream cheese and stir until smooth and creamy (I like to have the packages sit out for about 1/2 hr opened, just to help soften them). DON'T OVERBEAT
- Add sugar and mix until creamy

- Add sour cream, vanilla and salt and mix. Scrape the sides as you go
- On low speed, gradually add eggs (one at a time) until incorporated. Scrape the sides again.
- Fold in chocolate chips
- Pour into the springform pan.
- Transfer to center rack in your oven and bake at 325 for 75 min. Edges will look slightly puffy and light golden brown, and the center will spring back if you touch it.
- DO NOT OVER BAKE
- DO NOT OPEN OVEN DURING BACKING
- Remove from the oven and let cool for 10 min. Lose the crust from the inside of the pan with a knife and then loosen the pan (this will help prevent cracks as your cheesecake cools)
- Allow it to cool for 1-2 hrs before you transfer to the fridge
- Let it cool in there for 6 hrs min (best if over night).

CHAPTER SIXTEEN

the perfect ending

I could hear the whistle of the bomb from the moment Heather began with 'so, Wynne.'

When I heard the word 'Rich', I knew it was directly above me, and when she said 'single', that was when the bomb exploded.

I felt paralyzed for a split second. Complete and utter shock, mixed with a strong sense of disbelief.

Shock that this came out of nowhere.

Disbelief that she would go behind my back and get in touch with Rich. I felt myself becoming immersed within those feelings until, from the depths of my being, I managed to resurface and heard what she just said.

"You did what?" exploded out of my mouth. The disbelief and the beginnings of what I could only describe as outrage could be heard within those three words.

Heather just sat there calmly, nibbling on a breadstick while I felt like I was inside an out-of-control locomotive.

"I found Rich for you." She let another bomb drop and explode around me.

I couldn't believe I actually heard her say that.

"Why?" I asked her in stunned disbelief. "Why would you do

that?"

"One day, you are going to wake up from your dreams and realize it is all too late. I don't want that to happen to you. I love you. I'm your best friend. Why wouldn't I do this?"

I wanted to reach out and throw away the breadstick she nibbled on and then stomp on it.

"Um, maybe because I never asked you to. Or how about because you knew that I wouldn't want you to? Really, Heather, I can't believe you would go behind my back and do this," I answered her in even more disbelief if that was even possible.

"Okay. So, get over the shock, and realize what I originally said to you. Rich is still single. One hundred percent free to take if you so desire. No, I didn't tell him that you are looking, or even dreaming. I just casually said hi to him and asked him what was new." Heather took another sip of her fresh drink, but she wasn't done, I could see it in the way her lips tilted upward.

"Oh, and by the way, he said to say hi," she added.

Another bombshell just hit me.

He said to say hi. He actually thought of me enough to say hi to me.

A smile started to take place, if not on my face, because there was no way I was going to let Heather off the hook that easily, but definitely in my heart.

"Oh, you just casually said hi to him. How casual, Heather? Did you meet him on the street, bump into him and then realize who he was? Where did you see him, Heather? And why haven't you told me about this sooner?" I asked her. Something smelled just a bit fishy here.

"Well, casual enough," Heather admitted, albeit a little bit hesitantly. I knew it. I knew something wasn't right.

"No, don't look at me that way. I received a letter in the mail from the university asking for donations. I noticed his name as a teacher there, along with his email address. I just thought I would drop him a line and say hi. After all, we are old friends. I figured that if I could find out if he was still single or not, then I would know whether or not to encourage you to find him. You know he's the man in your dreams. You can't deny that. You still love him or at least hold onto the love you felt for him. What could it hurt to get in touch with him and see where it will lead? There's no 'significant' other in the picture, so what have you got to lose? And don't say your heart. I've heard that line one too many times lately. It won't work with me," Heather lectured.

"I'm not giving you a line, Heather. What if I'm not actually in love with the man, but rather with the idea of the man? In my dreams he might be Mr. Perfect, but in real life, he's probably far from it. My heart will get hurt, Heather. Hurt, because if it doesn't work out, then I have been living in fantasy land, being in love with the idea of a man," I confessed to her. I leaned forward onto the table and placed my head in my hands. It was hard to admit that to her.

Heather covered my hands with hers.

"Well, of course, you are in love with the idea. But don't you think it's time that you get a hold of the man and get to know him? I doubt very much that it would take long for you to quickly fall in love with the actual man instead of the idea."

I raised my head and glanced at Heather. She was giving me a sympathetic smile. She did understand what I was going through.

"I know you are right. But I am enjoying the idea. It's a lot safer," I admitted to her.

Heather began to laugh. Mama Rose was walking through the dining room and quickly came over to our table. Mama Rose glanced from Heather to me, shrugged her shoulders, and sat down. There's nothing Mama Rose likes better than to be with a crowd that laughs.

"Oh, Mama Rose. Wynne is trying to make me believe that she is a chicken. Can you believe that?" Heather continued to chuckle while shaking her head.

I glared at her, trying to silently portray that she needed to be silent. It was one thing to admit my weakness to my best friend. It was another to admit it to anyone else.

"Wynnie? The same girl who created a business out of nothing but sheer passion? Who was strong enough to hold her head high after being left at the altar? The same girl who isn't afraid to dine alone or to build her own dream home out of a run-down house? Not our Wynnie," Mama Rose mockingly exclaimed while holding both hands to her chest.

Mama Rose can be too cute at times. Especially when she tries to be serious when you know inside she is really laughing.

"Yes, that Wynnie," I said as I glanced at Mama Rose. "It's a whole lot easier to be strong in areas that don't affect the deep secrets in your heart," I told them.

"Well, of course, it is, my girl. But who do you think gives you that strength for those areas? The same one who will expose those deep secrets so you can be a stronger person. There is no secret that is too deep for the light of God to penetrate and expose. He will only expose those secrets for your benefit, not for your harm or for your humiliation. Too many people see their weaknesses as a hindrance in their lives. Instead, we need to see those very weaknesses as secret strengths. Imagine the things God can do through us when we surrender to him those areas that are the most protected," Mama Rose said softly to me while gently patting my hand.

I closed my eyes. Lifting my head high, I forced the tears that were threatening to escape to stay behind my eyelids. I'd just let them think I was praying while I tried to compose myself.

Sniffling, I gave Mama Rose a hug.

"You are so right, Mama Rose. Whatever would I do without you?" I ask her.

"Well, it would definitely make it easier to keep some of this weight off," Heather laughingly confessed while trying to hide her stomach to make a point. All three of us giggled.

"Now, I think it's time for my cheesecake, don't you think, Wynnie? Made special just for you," Mama Rose took a chunk of my cheek in her fingers and squeezed.

"I could never pass up your cheesecake. I think I'll even take a piece home to enjoy later on." I answered her with a grin on my face. I just knew she would have some cheesecake for me.

What a perfect way to end a very emotionally draining day.

CHAPTER SEVENTEEN

when reality hits, it hits hard

W hen I needed time to relax and reflect on all the chaos happening in my life, there was nothing I liked to do more than watch the sunrise.

With my mind whirling at a non-stop pace, sleep was just not happening. So with a cup of hot coffee in one hand and my Bible in my other, I headed out to my enclosed back porch, curled up in my blanket, and watched the sunrise.

Just as the sun began to peek over the horizon, you could see the mirror of that sun in all the tiny snowflakes covering my backyard. That morning the tiny flakes were swirling in the air due to a slight wind. Watching the shadows lift, the glorious colors appeared on the backdrop of God's canvas – it was all so beautiful. And so cold. It was a good thing my back porch was enclosed and heated.

There was just so much going through my head lately. From planning the engagement party to trying to avoid having to deal with some heart issues, and then feeling a little bit of excitement knowing that Rich was still single – I felt like I had lost focus on what is truly important in my life.

Watching a sunrise in the winter was so beautiful. I needed

some God time, and how could I not reflect on Him while watching His masterpiece fill the sky?

I had my bible opened to the book of Psalms. I liked to go through the book and find portions of scriptures that solely reflected on the majesty and awesomeness of God. When I did this, I found that all those issues that I keep fretting over became nonsense in the eyes of God. Yes, they were important, but saturating myself in the presence of God was even more so.

I tried to make it a habit to dwell on the praises of God while the sun roses, and then I allowed myself to deal with the issues of my heart. If I could get my priorities straight, then everything else would fall into line.

So with that in mind, I finished up my coffee, closed my bible, and let the tears fall.

Why exactly was I crying? Did I dare admit that deep in my heart, I felt hurt by God? Would I be struck with lightning if I said this out loud? Was it possible to feel this way about the one I can call Abba Father?

There was so much turmoil in my heart right then.

Why were we always told that we needed to surrender our uttermost desires to God? Why was I continually being reminded that 'my ways are not your ways, thus says the Lord of Hosts'?

Why did I need to give up my desires, when all I wanted was to be loved? I didn't want to be single. It wasn't a choice that I made on a daily basis.

I felt like I am paying for a past mistake, one that I made when I was too young to know my own heart. Was it really that terrible to desire a family? How much longer did I have to wait?

My internal clock was ticking away, and it's been ticking for a while now. If you loved me so much, God, then why didn't you bring someone into my life that I could love and will be loved in return?

I took a deep breath. There, I said it. Now what?

I closed my eyes and let my head drop toward my lap. I felt resigned. I knew in my heart I needed to let go of all that and move on. Find my joy in the Lord. I took another deep breath and prepared to completely surrender – for that day at least.

I got a picture in my mind's eye of my dream when I was on the beach. Of being held, hearing sweet words being whispered into my ear. I saw myself turning around and seeing the face of the man who was holding me. The same face that I saw on the website the other night. Rich Carradine. The true love of my heart. What did that mean? Was I just confusing what I wanted with what God wanted, or could he possibly be in my future?

I smiled and let the image play upon my thoughts for a bit until reality hit.

Reality hit hard. I had just finished pouring the last cup of coffee of the morning. I happened to glance at the clock and realized that it was Sunday, and I had missed the morning service.

Thinking back to what I just dealt with this morning, I decided not to feel guilty for playing hooky for once and decided this would be a good time to deal with other issues at hand.

The number one issue would be the party. My original thoughts were to hold off until this evening before I began to think about it, but then my thoughts and Nancy's thoughts were apparently on two different wavelengths.

Nancy Montgomery. The very lady my mother believed was gloating over the fact the jilted bride was holding an engagement party for the new bride.

Nancy, who wore a bright pink suit with black pants, walked up my front steps, knocked once on my door, and then proceeded to enter my home.

"Yoo-hoo. Anybody home?" she sang in a sweet disarming voice.

Thankfully, I was presentable. Could you imagine if Nancy entered my home like she did and I was standing there in my unmentionables?

If she saw me in my lounge clothes, I would be mortified. No one dared to bask in her presence unless they were dressed in their absolute best. That is just the way Nancy was; a refined social butterfly with horns sharper than a freshly sharpened pencil.

"Nancy – what a surprise. I'm in the kitchen," I called out to her as I quickly tidied up my messy kitchen.

I heard the clicking of her shoes as she came closer. I felt like I was about to face the firing squad in a few short seconds, so I took a deep breath, and then a huge sip of my coffee.

Unfortunately, the coffee didn't go down as smoothly as I had hoped, and so I ended up greeting my new guest by having a coughing fit. When I finally glanced up from being bent at the waist, I noticed not one but two sets of legs.

"Hello, ladies. Please excuse the mess, I wasn't exactly expecting company this morning," I said to my unexpected guests.

"Wynne. It's so nice to see you. Nancy insisted we had to talk to you, and when we saw you weren't at church this morning, we decided to just pop over here. I hope you don't mind?" Greeted the other guest to me, who turned out to be the newly engaged Stacey. Could my day get any better?

"Of course, she doesn't mind," interjected Nancy, cutting off my reply before I could even think of one. Perhaps it was a good thing Nancy spoke first.

I turned to Nancy, stood up straight, and decided to face her head on.

"Nancy, what can I do for you?" I asked her. I was polite and forceful, or at least that is how I hoped I sounded.

It was a good thing I spent some time with God that morning. Otherwise, I would not have had the grace and fortitude to deal with her.

"Well, seeing as you are planning a party for this Friday, I thought it might be best if we came over to help you in any way that you may need. I haven't heard from you yet concerning this, so naturally, you must need my help. It is only a few days away, you know. This is too important a party to leave every-thing until the last minute, dear." Nancy walked around my kitchen. She stopped in front of my large bay window facing out to my backyard. Thankfully, there was so much snow on the ground that she was unable to see the disarray that my garden was in. Fixing my gardens was definitely on my to-do list for the spring.

I decided to take the upper hand in all of this. After all, I wasn't the one marrying her son, so, therefore, I didn't have to deal with her on a regular basis.

"Oh Nancy, of course. I should apologize for not getting in touch with you sooner. And Stacey, that goes for you as well. I have had so much on the go that it completely slipped my mind. Of course, the mother of the groom and the bride-to-be would have a say in this party," I exclaimed. Was I pouring it on a little too thick, do you think? Nah.

"Now please don't worry at all. I have a group of ladies who are helping me with this, and everything is all set to go. Decora-tions are in order and very tastefully done, food has been dele-gated to various women, invitations are ready to be sent out, and there will even be an announcement in our town paper concerning the party. The church is booked, and flowers ordered. Everything down to the tiniest detail has been thought of and prepared." I counted off the lists on my fingers.

"Well, it certainly sounds like you have everything planned," Nancy said in a quiet voice. I think she was personally hoping to watch me stumble in this. Either that or perhaps she really wanted a hand in organizing the party.

"You can rest assured, Stacey, this will be a wonderful party," I addressed Stacey as she looked at me with a perplexing look on her face.

"Nancy, I am even making a special cheesecake and chocolate-dipped strawberries for Friday. I won't disappoint you, I prom-ise." I tried to make it sound more appealing. I was starting to feel a bit guilty for excluding them from the preparations. Perhaps I was wrong in wanting to do this without Nancy's domineering help.

"Here," I announced. "Why don't you take a seat at the table? I'll put on a fresh pot of coffee, and show you all the notes and pictures of what it will all look like?" I asked the two very quiet ladies.

Nancy composed herself quickly. I could see her stiffening up her spine, while Stacey let out an audible breath of relief. I think I managed to save the day.

"That would be lovely," replied Stacey as she took a seat at my small table. Thankfully, there was one space that was neither cluttered nor dirty.

After an hour of explaining and rehashing ideas and decisions, it ended up that both Stacey and Nancy were happy with not only the colors chosen but also with the flowers, food, and invitations.

While I was walking them to my front door, Stacey gave me a quick hug and thanked me for doing all of this. Nancy, of course, just walked out the door without a word, and I managed to close the door with enough dignity to last all of five seconds before I sank to the floor in front of my door in a puddle.

It was then that I noticed, that not only did I sink to the floor in a puddle, but I also sank right into a puddle of wet snow. Yuck. The perfect ending to a rather harried couple of hours.

CHAPTER EIGHTEEN
the email

My plan was to do a deeper dive into party planning for Friday, but the minute a notification came up that I had a new email from Rich, all thoughts of the engagement party dissipated from my mind.

I just stared at his name for a second, completely blanking everything else out. He wrote me. He actually wrote me.

His subject line reads: "With hopes from Rich."

Hopes? What type of hopes? That could only be a good thing, right?

My phone rang as I struggled to process something as simple as his subject line, and I answered on auto-pilot.

"Hello" I answered, still in somewhat of a daze.

"Wynne? Are you okay?" asked Heather on the other end. I guess she caught the tone of my voice – amazement combined with shock.

"What did you say to him, Heather?" I asked her. The shock still hadn't left my voice.

"Say to who? What are you talking about?" Heather asked. Now she was the one with the question in her voice.

"To Rich. What did you say to him, Heather? Please tell me," I begged. She had to have said something. Why else would he write me after five long years of silence?

"Wynne, take a deep breath. I already told you what I said to him, hon. What is wrong? Did something happen? Did you have another dream? Do you need me to come over?" Heather asked me in a bit of a panic.

"No, I don't need you to come over. Remember I had planned on having a nice relaxing day at home getting caught up? So far, that hasn't happened, but I'm not going to stop hoping that it does," I said to her a bit testily.

"Fine then. Geesh. What's going on?"

I closed my eyes. Did I really want to tell her? Maybe this was just a dream, and the email really wasn't there.

I opened my eyes. Nope, it wasn't a dream.

"I just received an email from Rich. After five years of silence and one year of you hounding me to contact him, I get an email from him. Why would he be writing me, Heather? Why now of all times?" I asked her with a hint of begging in that question.

"What does it say? Read it to me."

"I haven't read it yet, Heather. It's just sitting there in my inbox as an unopened new message. I'm not sure if I really want to open it. What if he just writes to say hi, and that's it? What do I say back?"

"What does the message title say?" Heather asked me in a quiet voice.

"With hopes from Rich," I answered her.

There was silence at the other end of the phone for a couple of seconds. Those seemed like the longest seconds of my life.

"With hope? With hope?" I could hear Heather mutter on the other line. "I think you should go ahead and open it. If he mentions hope, that has to be a good thing," Heather encouraged me.

"Well, of course, I'm going to open it. I think I need to be forti-fied with some chocolate first," I told her. There's no way that I could make it through this life-changing email without some chocolate.

"You and chocolate. Just hurry up and call me back. You can't leave me in suspense for too long, else you know what happens," she warned me.

Boy, was she right. Heather doesn't handle suspense very well. The last time I left her hanging for something less momentous than this, she left work early to come over and demanded to know what had happened.

Needless to say, although I'd hung up on her due to brownies being left too long in the oven, I learned my lesson about keeping things from her.

Rich's email was everything I'd hoped it would be.

SUBJECT: With hopes from Rich.

Surprise Wynne. Can you believe it has actually been almost five years since I last saw you?
I pray that this finds you well.
I spoke with Heather recently, and she mentioned how you have made your dreams become a reality. Good for you, Wynne. I'm so proud of you.
Heather also mentioned that you are not married (I'd been under the impression you were; otherwise, I would have been in touch sooner).
I know I'm being a bit presumptuous, but I am hoping that you will take the plunge with me: I miss you, Wynne.
I'm hoping you miss me too.
Sincerely, the same ole' Rich you once knew…

My heart raced, my stomach churned, and my throat was dry as a bone. Was this actually happening?

I replied before I faced reality and became too much of a chicken. I gave myself a quick pep talk – don't appear too anxious or eager; play it cool.

. . .

Dear Rich,

What a surprise. ~~It is so nice to hear from you.~~ Five years have gone by so fast, I'm sure we both have a lot to catch up on ~~like why neither of us are married~~. You always were better at taking those plunges than I was, but I'm game if you are.

From the girl with the same dreams as before, but who has changed more than you'd expect…Wynne

Short, concise, and definitely not as gushy as I could have been. Way back when, we used to personalize our signatures. Rich once told me that he looked forward to seeing how I would end my emails to him; he said he could catch a glimpse into my heart that way.

With the email written, all I needed to do was hit send, but I couldn't. I'd lost all the nerve and gumption. Was I ready for this? What if the dream I'd been holding onto burst with him back in my life? What if I'd been holding onto something that wasn't there?

But what if it was? What if there was still a spark between us?

Wasn't it better to find out than to live in the past?

I pressed the send button and immediately closed the lid of my laptop. I felt exhausted. Just one little action took so much emotional energy – I definitely needed another piece of chocolate now.

Tomorrow I'd start to diet.

CHAPTER NINETEEN
when dad visits

I had thoughts of starting the day off bright and early. I had my alarm set at a decent enough time to make some coffee and have a long shower. Perhaps try one of the muffins I took out of the freezer, spend some time with the kittens and then head to the store in a nice frame of mind.

Then the phone rang.

Even before I managed to squeak out a "good morning," I heard a demanding voice coming from the other line.

"What happened to you last night? Why didn't you phone me? Matt told me I had to wait until this morning to find out what happened with your email." Heather greeted me in her typical fashion – fast and furious.

"Seriously, I haven't even had my coffee." I knew I should have called her, but I wasn't ready last night.

All night I'd felt like I was living in a dream world. The thought that he wanted to renew our friendship, if nothing else, amazed me. I went to sleep with a smile on my face. My dreams were filled with romance, you know, the kind where you actually get to see the face of the man you are in love with.

"Tell me about the email already," Heather demanded.

I decided to tease her a bit. I knew just how much she hated that.

"Oh, you know, a little bit of this and a little bit of that. Nothing too serious, just hi, how are you, kind of thing." I told her with a 'who cares' type of voice.

"What do you mean 'that kind of thing'? Play nice here. I didn't bug you last night, and I could have."

That was true.

"Oh, all right. Tell you what. Meet me at the store, and I'll tell you all about it over fresh coffee and muffins," I told her. Just to keep the suspense a little longer.

"Some days....." I could hear the exasperation in her voice as she hung up. I did love to tease her.

The amount of snow outside was ridiculous, but I had the best neighbors who took care of my walkway and driveway in exchange for fresh baking on the weekends.

Thankfully, it wasn't too icy out as I walked to my car, arms laden with containers full of muffins and my idea book. The engagement party for Jude and Stacey was only a few days away. Hard to believe how quickly it had caught up with me.

I needed to finalize what everyone was bringing, the little things I might have forgotten, and make sure I incorporated all the ideas Nancy and Stacey wanted to be added.

When I pulled up to the store, I noticed Heather had already made it ahead of me. I chuckled as I tried to grab the muffins with one hand while twisting sideways to get out of my car. Without much thought, I swung both feet out of the car into the huge pile of snow right at the car door.

That's when I realized I still wore my slippers.

Just great. Now my feet were all soaked, and my hands were too full to do anything about the snow up my pants.

Heather held the door of the shop open for me, wisely remaining silent about my choice of footwear. With the muffin containers in one hand, I placed my one foot down on what I thought would be an ice-free sidewalk and quickly realized that it, in fact wasn't completely ice-free.

Not only did the muffins slide from my grip, but my foot followed suit along the ice-covered sidewalk, and I joined my muffins in the snow.

When I said that I joined the muffins in the snow, I mean that quite literally – I landed right on top of them. I looked up, hoping to find Heather there with a helping hand, but all I saw was her bent over at the waist laughing hysterically.

One hand was covering her mouth while the other one was half stretched out towards me, pointing towards the ground.

"Would you stop laughing and get over here? This isn't funny," I called to her. I tried to get up, but my foot kept slipping, and the muffins were in the way of me getting a firm grasp on the ground.

I glanced over at my would-be rescuer, and instead of finding her coming towards me, she was still stuck in the doorway laughing.

"HEATHER. THIS IS NOT FUNNY." I yelled while trying not to laugh. I was covered in snow, soaking wet, and sitting on a pile of muffins, unable to get up. Good thing those muffins were in containers, or else they would be mush by then.

"Oh, come on now, let me help you. I really hope those muffins aren't destroyed." Heather said as she finally left her post to help me.

"All you care about are the muffins?"

"Of course, silly. I forgot to eat breakfast." She blew me a raspberry as I plopped the muffins in her waiting arms.

She let out a small squeal as she opened the container. "Seriously, how did you know this was what I was craving?" She asked as I slid my way across the floor toward the back. Thankfully I kept a pair of shoes and extra clothing here in case of emergencies.

Just as I was about to close the bathroom door, Heather turned on the music, and wouldn't you know, a song about winter and snow and Christmas was playing. She gave me an innocent grin and then giggled at me. I glanced down at myself and saw puddles of snow forming at my feet where I stood.

"Just for that," I said to her, "you can clean up the floor."

It took me longer than I thought to clean myself up and look presentable. After drying myself off as best I could with the dryer in the bathroom, and then cleaning up my mess on the floor with paper towels, I walked out of the bathroom and could hear the doorbells jingle.

"Good morning, Sunshine." A booming voice greeted me. I instantly felt myself perk up and rushed over to the man who had just arrived.

"Dad. I've missed you. How are you feeling?" I asked him as I gave him a big hug.

My father is one of those blessings in my life that I continually thanked God for. Last year, he suffered a heart attack and I thought for sure that I had lost my father.

He has since semi-retired from being retired and has developed a habit of coming into the store a few mornings a week to start his day. He claims it's to try out my coffees before I poison the unsuspecting souls that come into my store each day. I personally think it is to get away from my mom for a few moments of solitude.

"Not too bad for being an old man, not too bad." He hugged me back, giving me an extra squeeze before he released me.

"Good to hear. Heather, put on the coffee this morning, so I can guarantee you that it's probably ruined already, but it's fresh," I said to him as we headed toward the coffee bar.

"Hey," said Heather. "I heard that. You're just jealous because you know Jack loves my coffee more than yours. Don't you?" She gave him a little punch on the arm.

"Now, now, girls," my dad admonished, "you both know how

I feel about your coffee. Why do you think I come in so often? Someone has to test it before you allow others to try it," he teased as he poured himself a cup of French Roast.

"You should really try one of our flavored coffees, Dad," I suggested.

"Now, why go and ruin a good thing?" He gave me a mock frown before grabbing two sugar packets.

I followed my dad to the corner table with the comfy chairs. This was exactly what I loved about my store: the coziness and comfort of feeling wrapped up in warmth while being surrounded by so many things that made me happy.

"So, how are you, Dad?" I asked him after a few moments of silence.

"Well, Sunshine, I'm doing all right. It's you I'm a little concerned about." He placed his mug down on the table.

"Oh, Dad, not you, too," I sighed.

"Yes, Sugar, me as well. I want to talk to you about something. This thing here that you gave your crazy mother permission to do was the most foolish thing you could have done," he admonished while picking up his coffee.

"What thing, Dad? I'm lost. What was wrong with that if you mean making some desserts for the party tomorrow?" I was a bit puzzled.

"No, not the desserts. You know your mother makes the best squares around. The only thing I ever complain about is she doesn't make enough for me to have." He pouted while taking a bite of his muffin.

"She's still keeping you on a tight leash, is she, Dad?"

"Well, she won't listen to me that a few sweets every once in a while can't hurt somebody," he complained.

"No, that wasn't what I was talking about, Wynne girl. This mystery date that she has lined up for you. That foolish thing."

"What mystery date, Dad?" I was even more puzzled now.

"What do you mean? You don't remember? The guy she has escorting you to the party Friday night, Wynne. That date. Don't tell me you don't remember giving your stubborn mother the heads up to do that," he cried out in exasperation.

Truth be told, I'd totally forgotten about it.

"It's fine. I made Mom promise not to get any notions in her head. Besides, I'm going to be so busy that I will hardly have any time for the guy on that night. I feel kind of sorry for him," I explained to him. I really didn't see it as that big of a deal.

"You have no idea, do you?" he asked me with a note of surprise in his voice.

"No idea about what? Dad, what is going on?" I asked him. Now I was starting to get a bit nervous.

"I promised your mother that I wouldn't ruin her surprise, and you know your mom. It'll be the end of me if I do. I just want to make sure that you are prepared for what she has done. This isn't a guy that you can brush off, Wynne," Dad warned me.

"Okay…" I wasn't worried before, but that quickly changed.

"I'm serious, Wynne. Do your old dad a favor, will you?"

"Anything." I'd do literally anything for him, and he knew that.

"Promise your old dad that you won't shrug this guy off. Please? Will you do that for me?" It was almost as if he was begging me.

"Okay, Dad. I promise. I'll wear my best outfit and dazzle him with my smile. I'll make Mom so happy that she will be floating. In return, I want you to promise me something, Dad." I said to him.

This was going to be a give-and-take situation. If I had to give a lot to some guy that my mom felt was 'right' for me, then he was going to have to give as well.

"I knew you would try to bargain with this. All right, what do I have to promise?" he replied in a tone of resignation.

"I want you to promise me that you will come to the party with Mom. Now, don't shake your head at me. Jude is not the bad guy here, Dad, and it's time you let up on being protective of me with this. I mean it, Dad. It's been three long years, Dad, and you need to forgive him for hurting your little girl. Please?" I begged him.

My dad was a wonderful man, very loving, generous, and funny. But watch out if you hurt someone he loved. All bets were off then, and he became very protective.

He blamed everything on Jude for the past three years. I, of course, have never told him the truth, but I have tried to get him to let it all go.

"Wynne, don't get into this. You already know how I feel about Jude. The least he could have done was act man enough and stick around to help clear up the mess instead of running like a ninny, making you deal with it all," Dad said with extra gruff voice in his voice.

"It wasn't his fault," I found myself whispering.

"Of course, it was his fault, honey. Stop taking the blame for him," his voice rose ever so slightly.

I dropped my head and stared at the floor. Enough was enough. It was time I finally spoke the truth.

"No, Dad. It wasn't his fault. It was because of me the wedding was called off. I broke his heart."

For the past three years, I'd let him blame Jude. Why? I didn't want to appear less than in his eyes. I wanted to be his perfect little girl, and witnessing the look of disappointment in his gaze at my failure was something I never wanted to experience.

So I lied. I kept silent and let him blame Jude.

I lifted my head slightly to look at my father. He was just sitting there in stunned silence. Neither one of us said anything for a few moments, yet it felt like an eternity.

"Are you telling me that you were the one to call off the wedding?" he asked with a hint of incredibility in his voice.

I shook my head. "It was a mutual decision. Jude asked me to give him something that I couldn't give. He wanted my whole heart, and I couldn't give that to him. You can't fault him for taking off like he did," I admitted to him in a catchy voice.

Part of me was relieved to finally admit I'd been at fault, but the other felt shame for letting him down.

"So you were still in love with that Richard guy from school. Is that what you are really saying? I thought you got over him. Why wouldn't you tell me this before now? I'll love you no matter what, you know that." There was a wrenching sound in my father's voice as he told me he loved me.

I took a deep sigh and raised my head.

"I just didn't want to disappoint you, Dad," I whispered.

My father appeared to be choked up for a few moments.

"Ah, Wynne, honey – you will never be a disappointment to me," he said as he took my hand in his and lightly rubbed it.

So that was how receiving a father's love felt. Like, you were surrounded by warmth, acceptance, and love. Knowing that no matter what, that love will never change. Almost like a little girl who climbs up into her daddy's lap, knowing that she would always receive love from her daddy.

I'd been afraid of admitting the truth because I didn't want him to be disappointed in me. I was afraid to admit the truth, to face the consequences…which would also explain so much about me.

I could face anything and be willing to fail when it came to anything but my heart. Everyone called me courageous and bold for pursuing my dreams, but if only they knew the truth.

The truth was that I wasn't courageous or strong. I was weak and fearful. I preferred to live in the past, in my dreams, rather than have my heart broken again.

It was easier to live in the dream of 'what if' instead of embracing the reality of it.

It was easier to blame others for the failures rather than accept I needed to forgive myself for my part in those failures.

Ouch.

While I was silently contemplating this new thought, I heard my father talking under his breath.

"So your mother isn't that much of a nutcase after all, then."

"Pardon me?" I asked him.

"Hmm, oh, nothing honey, just talking to myself," he replied.

With that, he stood up, drank the last bit of his coffee, and prepared to leave.

"Now you just remember what you promised me. I think you'll find that you may just like your mystery man after all," he chuckled as he hugged me.

I felt a bit puzzled, and I'm sure I had the facial expressions to show it, but dad just gave me a quick wave and left the store whistling a tune.

"What was that about?" Heather asked.

"I have no idea," I confessed. "One minute, everything was serious, and then the next, he's chuckling and saying weird things about my mom."

"Sometimes I wonder about your family." Heather shook her head.

I just stuck my tongue out at her.

"It takes one to know one," was my sassy reply.

"And wouldn't you know?" Heather shot back at me while grabbing my hand. She quickly tugged me back into the chair that I had just vacated and pushed me down.

"Now, before another person enters this store, I want to hear about that email." Heather stood above me with her hands on her hips.

"Someone's getting a wee bit pushy, aren't they?"

"Wynne," Heather growled at me.

"All right, all right, sit down, and I'll let you in on what he said," I said soothingly to her in hopes of placating her.

As I proceeded to tell Heather all that Richard had written to me, we had two customers come into the store. Heather glanced up and told the ladies that we would be with them soon, making me finish my story.

Amidst her little squeals when I told her what he wrote and her little giggles when I confessed my extra need for chocolate when I sent my reply, I managed to get the whole story out in time to speak to the customers that continued to arrive despite the amount of snow that continued to add up on the piles already formed on the ground.

Time to put on more coffee and get the Christmas music started.

wynne's cinnamon streusel muffins

Muffins. They are cupcakes without the icing and oh so delicious! Cinnamon Streusel are probably my favorite to snack on...heat it up a little and add a dab of butter and I'm lost. What is it about cinnamon desserts that keep calling...I'm not sure, but either way, you will love these! (If you like coffee cake, you'll love this)

WYNNE'S CINNAMON STREUSEL MUFFINS

CINNAMON STREUSEL INGREDIENTS:

- 1/2 cup flour
- 1/4 cup brown sugar
- 1/2 tsp cinnamon
- 3 tbsp butter (cut into pieces)

MUFFIN BATTER INGREDIENTS:

- 1/2 cup butter (softened)
- 1 cup sugar
- 2 eggs
- 1/2 cup milk
- 2 tsp vanilla
- 2 cups flour
- 2 tsp baking powder
- 1/2 tsp salt

STEPS:

- Preheat oven to 375 and line muffin tin with cups
- In medium blow, mix streusel ingredients, cutting in the butter, until it resembles small chunks size of peas
- Place this in the fridge
- In a large bowl (or stand), cream butter and sugar until light and fluffy
- Add eggs one at a time
- Add milk and vanilla
- Add flour, baking powder and salt until combined
- Use 1/4 cup to fill muffin liners
- Sprinkle crumb topping, pressing into the batter slightly
- Bake for 20-22 min

CHAPTER TWENTY

party planning

C razy upon crazy was how my day continued.
With all the morning mishaps and busyness, I should
have clued in that the day would not get any better, no matter
how much chocolate I consumed.

Thankfully, the store stayed quite busy during the morning, so
I didn't have time to ponder my father's bizarre behavior and
request.

Unfortunately, that also meant I was unable to focus on the
party at all. With less than a month to Christmas, I couldn't keep
my shelves stocked - which wasn't a bad thing.

My goal was to give people ideas apart from the normal bath
towels, kitchen gadgets, and plates. Instead, they came into
Chocolate Blessings Cafe and found an assortment of wall décor,
interesting table pieces, one-of-a-kind ornaments, and handmade
items.

Things were so crazy we even ran out of the roses we handed
out - before lunch, something that rarely ever happened. In fact, I
could count how many times that had happened. I had to wait till
Lily came in for her afternoon shift to grab more from the florist
next store.

My day just got better the moment Jude and Stacey walked in. They were disgustingly sweet together and so very much in love with all the loving glances, little touches, and the fact that they stuck to each other's side like glue, it was kind of hard not to notice.

I didn't want to look but couldn't help myself. Every time she reached for something with her left hand, that ring of hers sparkled and with each sparkle, a knife in my gut twisted.

Was I jealous? Yes. The second I realized that I whispered a prayer for forgiveness because jealousy was an ugly sin, or so my mom used to say whenever I complained that I lived in hand-me-downs instead of getting new jeans or sneakers.

That ring. The smiles on their faces. The cute glances they would give each other...I wanted to bolt from the room with some excuse but I didn't. I was better than that. Better than a jealous ex-fiance, right?

"All right, you two lovebirds," I called them over to me. "Let me see that ring."

Did I want to see it? No. Yes. No. Gah.

"Wynne. Isn't it gorgeous?" Stacey gushed while extending her arm, so her ring was right in front of my face. Honestly, she could have kept the ring at her side, and I still would have seen the beauty of it.

"It's beautiful." The words slipped from my mouth with a softness I didn't expect. I don't think Jude did either, from the look he gave me.

I felt the tears build, and that wasn't going to do. I'd cried enough over this man, over our relationship...I was not going to cry one more tear, especially not with everyone watching me.

When Jude proposed to me, he gave me his grandmother's heirloom ring with the promise that he would buy me a ring deserving of his love later on. It wasn't fancy. It wasn't shiny. It definitely wasn't the size of the ring on Stacey's hand, either.

The one he gave me was a simple band with a small diamond.

The one on Stacey's finger was pearl shaped, one large diamond surrounded by smaller ones. A stunning piece that spoke volumes about their love.

I had to turn away with some ridiculous excuse about needing to make a fresh pot of coffee, but it wasn't long before Jude was at my side.

"Um, Wynne," Jude shuffled his feet as he waited for me to look at him.

I really didn't want to. Petty, I know, but I didn't want him to see the longing on my face for what wasn't mine. Not the ring, but what it signified.

"Hey," I finally said as I turned with what I hoped was a gentle smile on my face. "That ring is amazing, and I'm very happy for you both."

"Thanks. It's nothing like my grandmother's, but I didn't think it would be right to give her that, especially after…well, you know? Maybe one day I'll have a daughter I can pass it down to." He lifted his shoulder in a slight shrug while peaking glances over at Stacey.

"Listen, about Friday night," he continued, "I just want to say thank you. I know the whole situation isn't ideal, but you've really outdone yourself in planning this for us." Jude twiddled his thumbs.

"Ideal? I can't tell you the number of people who have asked me what I was thinking to offer. I mean…" I let out a sigh and shrugged. "It's fine. Odd, different, very un-traditional, but hey…" I let the words fall between us, any other explanation was unnecessary.

"Yeah, um, listen, you're um…" he paused, as if he struggled to spit the words out.

"Yes?"

"Well, your dad came by this morning to apologize."

My brows rose toward my hairline at that. "Oops."

"I thought we had agreed not to tell anyone about what

happened, especially our parents. I'm not upset, but the least you could have done was warn me. My mom heard us talking, and now she wants to have a talk with me," Jude told me in an agitated voice. Good to see I wasn't the only one who cowered before his or her mom.

"I'm sorry. I didn't...it just..." now I was the one tongue-tied. "It just came out this morning. I didn't want him to blame you anymore for something that wasn't even your fault," I confessed.

"It's all right. It was just a bit awkward. I mean, your dad apologized to me when really it should have been me apologizing to him," Jude stated.

"Well, I guess it's out of the bag now. I had to tell my dad, you're going to have to deal with your mom. However, I wouldn't wish that on my neighbor's dead cat." I smiled at the way he quirked his lips. "Listen, it's in the past, history. Let's not rehash this again, okay?"

I was tired of dealing with all this. I felt like I'd been rung inside out dealing with all the emotional baggage toward my dad, God, and myself. Enough is enough.

"Plus, about tomorrow – really, it's no big deal. There are enough people involved with this now that it really isn't me putting on this party for you and Stacey. It's basically become a church event. So the people you need to thank are those that loved you and taught you about Jesus your whole life," I told him.

"Are you sure?" Jude asked.

"Absolutely positive. Now go and stand beside your fiancée before she notices that you are gone." I pushed him away with my hands.

I waited until I knew he was gone before my shoulders sagged. I was ready for the day to be over so I could climb under a warm blanket, play with my kittens and ignore the rest of the world for a little bit.

"So, tell me what you really feel." I heard a voice behind me say.

I literally jumped with a shriek and all the to-go cups and lids went sliding everywhere.

"Aggh, Heather. Do you have to sneak up behind people like that?" I swatted her arm.

"In order to get the truth in a timely fashion with you, yes, as a matter of fact, I do," Heather replied saucily to me as she swatted me back.

"Don't you know it's rude to eavesdrop?" I replied.

"When has that ever stopped me?" Heather asked.

"Hmm, now that is true." We both laughed.

Lily came to clean up, so Heather and I both grabbed a fresh cup of coffee and went to sit in the back office to chat. Much to my surprise, the office was already occupied.

"Well, hey there, stranger," I said to Matt.

He had somehow managed to slip past me this morning without my even noticing. He looked happy as he sat back in the desk chair surrounded by mounds of paper and a half-full cup in his hand.

"Guess Heather forgot to mention I was back here, eh?" He gazed adoringly at his wife.

"Are you having fun?" I asked him as I glanced down at the papers on the desk.

"You betcha. We're actually doing really well this month," Matt informed me.

In all the craziness, it slipped my mind that today was book-keeping day. It did feel great to hear how well we were doing.

"We're not normally this low on stock, though, are we? Or have you just been filling up the shelves?" Matt pointed towards the depleting stock that we had sitting on the shelves behind him.

Low stock was both a good and bad issue to deal with. "A little of both," I admit. "With planning this party, I guess I got behind. Sorry. I don't think it will be a problem, though. I'm expecting a box to come any day with some great Christmas items and more candles." I peeked in the boxes to see what we have left.

I glanced up to find Heather in her husband's lap, whispering sweet nothings in his ear.

"Gag," I teased.

They both rolled their eyes at me. "I'm being tasked with grabbing lunch. You girls have a good chat, and please make sure you're done by the time I get back." Matt zipped up his jacket and walked toward the door.

"What did you say to him?" I asked her as we both sat down.

"Oh, just that we needed to have a girly chat and that I was craving some Chinese food." She winked. Since being married, I've noticed that Matt and Heather seem to have their own personal language that I don't understand at all.

"So what were the magic words, girly chat or Chinese food?" I asked her.

Heather just laughed at me.

"So, are you really doing okay?" she asked me, ignoring my earlier question.

That was the hint that it was time for some serious talk now. I took a sip of coffee and laid my heart bare before her.

"Crazy enough, I think I'm fine. I've been having some real heart-to-heart discussions with God, and I think admitting to my dad what happened with Jude really helped." I had to close my eyes and force the swell of tears from overflowing. Gah. I hated crying, especially in public. I'm an ugly crier - red, swelling nose and all.

"When my dad told me that he would never be disappointed in me, it was like a huge weight lifted off of my shoulders. I believe it also opened up a section of my heart that I've been hiding from God as well," I confided.

"Wow. That's great. You know, whenever Pastor talks about the Father's love on Sundays, he often mentions that our views of God as our Father, or Abba come from our relationships with our earthly fathers," Heather reminded me in an encouraging way.

"I thought of that as well. I used to think that we could separate the two if we really wanted, but I don't think that is possible. How we respond and react with our own fathers really does control how we respond to God as our heavenly father." I admitted to her.

She smiled. "Let's not forget the fact that you received an email from a good-looking dream guy. That always helps to heal the heart." The smile on her face was quite cheeky.

She knew me so well.

"Speaking of a handsome dream guy, did you dream about him last night by any chance?" Heather asked with a sly gleam in her gaze.

"No. Isn't that funny? I thought for sure I would, especially after receiving his email. But it was just a deep, peaceful sleep for me last night." I'd never even noticed my dreamless sleep this morning.

"Hmmm, I wonder what that means?"

"Oh, you." I knew she was just teasing me. I could tell Heather had more on her mind, but thankfully, Matt knocked on the door and poked his head in at the perfect time.

"Is it safe to enter now? I brought goodies." Matt waved a bag of Chinese food in the air.

"As long as you come bearing food, come on in," I called out to him.

I glanced over at Heather in time to see her give a little pout and then glanced quickly back at Matt and saw him shrug. Hmm, I wondered what was going on between these two.

After a delicious lunch of chicken fried rice, chicken balls, beef stir fry, and an egg roll, I spent the afternoon replacing our depleting stock. Knowing that Lily would stay until closing, I felt fairly confident that I would be leaving the store in good hands. With teasing remarks to watch out for the snow, Heather and Matt pushed me out the door.

Watching carefully where I stepped on my way to the car, I found myself wishing that Richard had written me back already. I felt like a silly little schoolgirl waiting to receive her first love note from a boy, giddy and foolish.

I loved this feeling; it was new yet comfortable, like an old pair of sneakers. I had no idea where this feeling was going to lead me, but I really hoped I could be like Dorothy following the yellow brick road.

The first thing I did at home was to get into comfort mode: comfy yoga pants, hoodie, thick fuzzy socks, and my hair in a bun. I then went on the hunt for the kittens.

Since adopting them, I've come to the realization they are pirates. They like to steal treasure and hide it away in a box at the back of my closet.

"All right you two, where are you?" I was down on my knees, pushing clothes, shoes and bags out of the way and found them both curled up in the box. I wish I had my phone on me, I'd have taken a picture.

I slipped my hoodie around until the hood was in the front and cradled both kittens inside it. They barely woke up as I gingerly walked through the house to the table where my laptop waited.

I was on a mission...to order more goods for the store. First things first though, I eagerly checked my inbox.

Sure enough, the message that I was hoping for had arrived. Tiny flutters of hope swished in my stomach as I took a second to open the email.

What would he say? What would happen next?

My dreaming Wynne,
You always had the best dreams. Good to know that hasn't changed. Do you remember how we'd meet for coffee and talk about our dreams? We should do that again. I hear you serve a mean cup of Joe at your place.
I'm so proud of you for following your dreams. I want to do that too - and in fact, God is opening doors in ways I never thought

possible. I'm a run-and-jump type of guy…if I hold on to your hand tight enough, will you jump with me? I know - bold talk, especially since we haven't chatted in a long time, but…I won't let another five or more years go by.

I'll hold tight, I promise – Rich

It was like someone just handed me a gift box and said everything and anything I've ever wanted is inside…and all I needed to do was take it.

It couldn't be that easy, right? Was Richard the man I'd been waiting for? Was he the man in my dreams? My soul mate?

In my heart, the answer was yes to all the questions. Yes, it could be that easy. Yes, he was the man I'd waited for. Yes, he was the man I'd been dreaming about. Yes, he was my soul mate.

I called Heather. If I were off base, she'd be the one to tell me.

"When God opens the doors, He opens all the windows too. This is awesome. That part about your coffee…was that him hinting at an invite?"

Honestly, I hadn't thought about that. "Maybe? Should I?" No, no, I shouldn't. Well, I could…just throw it out there and see what he said. No harm, no foul, that was the saying, right?

"Of course, you should. Why wouldn't you?"

Why wouldn't I? I had so many reasons but they all sounded like pithy excuses.

"You probably don't need to, now that I think about it. Richard is the type that, once he decides what he wants, he goes after it in full force. Or have you forgotten that about him?" Heather asked me.

True. Very very true. "People can change, you know," I told her. What if he decided that running wasn't the best option and he wanted to go slow? Not that slow was a bad thing, but…

"Snap out of it. You know …" Heather stopped, and in the background, I could hear Matt's voice.

"I, ah, I need to go. Matt needs me. Bye."

My nerves were all jangled up and if I let myself, I could have sat there for hours daydreaming about the past, about Rich, about what could be…but I had stock to buy and a party to plan.

Then I'd let myself dream…

CHAPTER TWENTY-ONE

secret admirer

With the engagement party coming up fast, my hours flew by in a rush and I was in a constant state of chaotic catastrophes.

To start with, more people than expected were coming to the party. Which meant, there was not enough food, drinks, or anything...which also meant the night would be a disaster, which I couldn't let happen.

I sat at my kitchen table, fingers yanking hair out of my head, trying to figure out how to get more food and beverages without asking people to donate, when my phone rang.

"You're wasting away, everyone tells me. Come for dinner tonight." In typical form, Mom demanded rather than asked. And as much as I loved her homemade cooking, I wasn't up to the grilling about to come.

"Who says I'm wasting away? If anything, my pants are too tight from all the desserts I've been eating."

"Everyone."

"Well, everyone was wrong. As much as I'd love to come for dinner, tonight's not the best night. This party was falling apart and I don't know how to fix it."

"I heard. Don't argue with me. Bring your notebook and we'll figure things out after you eat my lasagna. Two minds are always better than one. Besides, you know how much I love parties," Mom said, trying to twist my arm into coming.

Hmmm, my mother's lasagna. How could I turn that down? "Do you want me to bring dessert?" I asked her.

"No need, I already made my chocolate cake. Go have your bath and then come on over. Make sure you turn off your phone during your bath," she told me.

I laughed. "Good idea," I said.

"Well then, what are you doing still on the phone?"

I shook my head as I hung up. She was definitely a unique individual that kept me on my toes. Our relationship was complicated but grounded in love, and I wouldn't have it any other way.

I managed to scoot out the kittens from playing with the toilet paper in the bathroom and filled up the tub. I always keep a large selection of bath items in a basket on the cupboard. Vanilla and coconut were my go-to. With the phone turned off and bubbles in the tub, I lit the candles and went to find the latest romance that I was reading.

No chocolate tonight – I needed to keep room for the lasagna and Mom's cake. I don't know how she does it, but she makes the best chocolate cake I've ever tasted, and no matter how hard I attempt to recreate her recipe, it never tastes the same.

So much for that diet I wanted to start.

I arrived at my parent's home just in time to see a florist van pulling away and Mom standing at the door, holding a large arrangement of flowers. She casually looked at the card before placing it in her apron pocket.

"Those are beautiful flowers, Mom. Who are they from?" I asked her as I bent slightly to smell the bouquet.

My father walked up behind me, placed his arm casually around my shoulders, and asked the same question.

"Who sent you flowers, dear?" he asked her as he tried to see if there was a card to read.

"Oh, you know, just a secret admirer," Mom announced as she smiled and gave my dad one of those secret looks shared between couples.

My father wrinkled his forehead as he tried to think.

"Secret admirer? Who would be sending you ... oh ... a secret admirer," he said with a hint of secrecy in his voice.

All right, now I was intrigued.

"Why do you have a secret admirer, Mom?" I asked.

"Why does anyone have a secret admirer, dear?" She said in a faraway tone as she walked into the kitchen. I gave my father a look, but he shrugged his shoulders and headed into the living room, where I could hear the low-volume tone of the television.

I listened for a few seconds and then heard the common gunshots of a western show being played. I smiled, knowing that some things never change. Nine times out of ten, if I were to drop by, Mom would either be in the kitchen or garden, and my father would have his cowboy movies on.

"Is there anything I can do to help?" I asked Mom. She was unwrapping the arrangement, a soft secretive smile on her face.

"Just tell your dad to turn the television off. Dinner is on the table." She placed the arrangement on the kitchen island.

As we all gathered at the table, I saw she'd outdone herself yet again: hot lasagna cooling to the side, garlic bread fresh from the oven, and homemade Caesar salad.

"This looks delicious, Mom." I started to fill my plate after my father said grace.

"I wanted to spoil you a little bit. You've had a lot on your plate, and I'm worried about you." Mom reached for my hand.

"You don't have to worry about me. I'm fine, I promise."

She held my hand tight, and the look on her face had me turning toward Dad who only stared down at his plate.

That's when I knew.

"You told her." No sense in asking. He looked as guilty as a kid with his hand caught in the cookie jar.

He stuffed his mouth with a bite of garlic bread and wouldn't look me in the eye.

"Your father didn't have to tell me anything," Mom said, giving my hand a pat before she released it. "Do you honestly think I wouldn't have figured it out? It might have taken me a while, but a mother always knows her daughter's heart." She tsk-tsk'd me before she picked up her knife and cut into her lasagna. "I knew you were keeping a secret. You were too calm and defensive of Jude to be the jilted bride. I wish you had told me though. Let me tell you, I didn't appreciate getting a call from Nancy with no warning."

Lovely. Just lovely.

"Mom," I sighed, "what did Nancy have to say when she called?" I should have known that this was more than a simple dinner invitation.

"Oh, you know, Nancy. It takes a lot for her to apologize, but she said that she was sorry for allowing something as trivial as our children's problems to get in the way of our friendship. I told her that as mothers, our children always came first and that our friendship never deteriorated; it was just on hiatus for a while," Mom explained.

"So that means … what exactly?" I asked.

"Well, we are going for coffee sometime next week. I'll let you know so you can reserve a table for us at your shop. Now, enough of all this nonsense. Enjoy your dinner." Mom patted my hand and focused on her food.

"But …" I began. My father gave his famous "harrumph" before I could say anymore.

That was his way of letting me know to let things alone.

I helped clean up the kitchen after dinner while dad went back to the living room to have his usual post-dinner snooze. I was trying to work up the courage to explain myself when my mom turned to me.

"It's taken you three long years to admit to your father and me what really happened that day in the church. It hurt my heart to know that you didn't trust us enough with the truth. We would have supported you no matter what. But as it was, you left us in the dark and let your father hold a grudge against a man that didn't deserve it." She pursed her lips.

"Now, I figured out awhile ago that Jude wouldn't have left you that day if it weren't for something that was important. I just wish you had come to me. Your father and I have had a long talk, many times actually, about all of this. He wouldn't believe me until he heard it from your mouth. I'm not saying this to make you feel guilty. I love you." She reached her arms out to me. "You are the daughter of my heart and my blood. I just want you to know that we are always here for you and that you are never alone, no matter how high you like to build the walls around your heart."

I rushed over and welcomed the feel of her arms around me. The tears streamed down my face and soaked her shirt.

"You're right, Mom. I should have told you guys from the beginning. I was afraid of being a disappointment to you," I confessed.

"Oh, honey. When will you realize just how proud of you we are? You are such a gift from the Lord, and look at all that He has blessed you with. You will never be a disappointment to us." Mom held me by the shoulders.

"Now, it's time we put this all behind us and celebrate with chocolate cake," Mom said loud enough to wake my father.

"What are we celebrating?" Dad shouted back from the living room. I could hear the squeak of his chair as he stood.

"Life, love, and new happiness," Mom declared as he walked into the kitchen and placed his arms around her waist.

"Any excuse is a good excuse when it comes to your cake," Dad replied with a twinkle in his eye.

And people often wonder whom I inherited my love for chocolate from.

mom's mouthwatering chocolate cake recipe

Who doesn't love a moist (sorry for the word...) chocolate cake! It's decadent, mouthwatering and you can't help but eat it from the cake stand or pan by the forkful (well, at least, I can't help but eat it like that...seriously, chocolate cake never lasts around me).

MOM'S MOUTHWATERING CHOCOLATE CAKE RECIPE

CAKE INGREDIENTS:

- 1 3/4 cup flour
- 2 cups sugar
- 3/4 cup cocoa powder
- 2 tsp baking soda
- 1 tsp baking powder
- 1 tsp salt
- 1 cup buttermilk (when Ina Garten says to use buttermilk, you listen!)
- 1/2 cup oil
- 2 eggs (room temperature)
- 1 tsp vanilla
- 1 cup hot coffee

BUTTERCREAM ICING INGREDIENTS:

- 6 ounces semisweet chocolate (use the cooking bars, not the chocolate chips)
- 1 cup butter
- 1 egg yolk (room temperature)
- 1 tsp vanilla
- 1 1/4 cup icing sugar

LET'S MAKE THE CAKE:

1. Preheat oven to 350
2. Butter 2 8" round cake pans
3. Sift flour, sugar, cocoa, baking soda, baking powder and salt together and add to bowl
4. Combine on low until mixed
5. In a separate bowl - add buttermilk, oil, eggs and vanilla
6. Slowly add wet mixture to dry mixture - keep the speed low and scrape the sides and bottom as you go
7. Add the coffee, slowly, and mix
8. Pour into the pans and bake for 35-40 min

9. Cool in pans for 30 min, then turn onto cooling rack and cool completely
10. Then add the icing to the cake, one layer at a time

TO MAKE THE ICING:

1. Chop the chocolate and melt it (microwave slowly or use a heatproof bowl over simmering water, stirring until it's all melted)
2. Beat the butter until it's light and fluffy (3 min)
3. Add egg yolk and vanilla and beat another 3 min
4. With mixer on low - gradually add icing sugar until it's all mixed well. Increase speed and scrape the bowl as necessary

This was a cake recipe I've had forever, but when I discovered the Barefoot Contessa and the secret of the buttermilk and then adding the egg yolk to the icing...blew my mind and it's now my favorite recipe to use

I think it will be yours, too.

CHAPTER TWENTY-TWO

too many secrets

"Let's figure this party out." Mom pushed aside her empty cake plate and reached for my notebook.

I was pretty proud of that notebook and everything it contained. It had all the details, down to images of color palettes and centrepiece ideas.

Every single detail and thought I'd had about the party was in that book - without it, I'd be a lost cause.

"Back when I organized these parties at the church, I was never this organized. You certainly didn't get that gene from me," Mom said as she went through my pages.

"Not everyone likes the 'fly by the seat of your pants' arrangement like you, Mom." She had a tendency to live her life with the assumption that everyone else knew exactly what she was thinking, and that everything would either work out or it wouldn't.

According to her, it always worked out.

"Oh, shush you. You certainly have all your ducks in a row. Why are you so stressed?"

I turned to the last page, where I had all the numbers written down.

Her brows slowly rose to her hairline, and her lips puckered up like she'd eaten a sour candy.

"So we bring extra food. The church has more than enough supplies for the rest. You're stressing about nothing."

Stressing about nothing? Did she even hear herself?

"You, my darling girl, have a tendency to focus on the wrong issues. Something else is going on, isn't there? Is it the store? Your finances? You know I'm here to listen."

Store? Finances? No, all of that was fine. Mom was right though, I was stressing about something in my control, rather than the one thing I have no control of.

My love life. I couldn't tell her that.

"It will all be fine, I promise. I'll chat with some ladies, and we'll make up some extra veggie and dessert trays, all right? Don't forget, I already have a crew set up to meet at the church Friday after lunch. Everything will be fine," Mom walked over to her 'to do' list on the fridge and read the names of those helping to set up the room.

She was right. Of course, she was right. I was stressing over appetizers when the focus of this party was anything but the food.

"Which reminds me," Mom said as she packaged up leftovers for me to take home. "You haven't forgotten about your date, right?"

I really hoped she didn't see my eye roll. "Friday night is probably not the best night for a blind date, Mom." I couldn't believe I let her talk me into that in the first place.

"Why? I think it's the perfect night. You'll pay attention to someone other than the newly engaged couple. I thought you'd be happy?"

There was so much more I wanted to say, that I could have said, but one look at Mom's face and I knew it wasn't worth it.

That was probably why I agreed to this ridiculous idea in the first place. It wasn't worth the argument.

"He's meeting me at the church, right? I'll be there early, so it only makes sense. He can pitch in and help set up the tables and chairs."

"At the church? I already gave him directions to your house," she whined to me while she wrung her hands. Oh-oh, not a good sign.

"Mom, meeting at my house just isn't going to work. I won't even be there. Plus, considering I don't even know him, don't you think meeting in public is a better idea? Please, can you rearrange whatever plans you made for me?"

My mom studied the ceiling as she muttered a little while creating a new plan.

"You're right. Meeting at the church is a great idea," she finally said, with a sense of contentment in her voice.

"Great. I appreciate that, Mom. Please remember, though, that this date is only for one night – no other promises," I reminded her. I should have also said it was a one-time event too. I don't need my mother to set me up on blind dates, *thank-you-very-much*.

"Oh, I know. No promises. I don't really think that will be such a big deal once you meet him face to face," she said with a little too much assurance in her voice.

Now I was worried.

"Please don't tell me this is some long-lost cousin's best friend or a son from some old buddy of Dad's, right? You've met this guy? Can vouch for him? He wasn't someone you found off a dating app, or something?"

"A dating app? You should know me better than that."

Which was why I asked. Did I think she would go on an app and find someone for me? No. But did I think she had a friend who would do it?

One hundred percent.

"You owe me," I warned her as I wiggled my way into my coat and boots and took the bag of food containers she held for me.

"That's what you'll be saying after Friday, trust me. Good night, darling. Sweet dreams." Mom closed the door.

Sweet dreams. What did she know that I didn't? Did Heather talk to her? She wouldn't have…right?

I tried not to think about it as I drove home, pushed the party, the blind date, and everything out of my mind, and focused instead of replying to Rich.

I'd decided I was going to do a casual invite to the store. That didn't make me look too desperate but showed my interest. A win-win, in my books.

I'd eat more of the cake and enjoy a relaxing evening...at least, that had been the plan until I walked into my home and was hit in the face with the smell of something burning.

I dropped everything and ran inside. Had I left a candle burning? Where the kittens okay? I'd closed them in my spare bathroom, so they couldn't have gotten out, right?

Wrong.

So very, very wrong.

I must have forgotten to turn off my coffee machine, which explained the burnt smell.

But the mess could only be blamed on my two small housemates, who apparently had escaped from the bathroom.

Flowerpots were knocked over, with soil tracking all through the kitchen, tiny cat prints leading the path. The Tupperware of cinnamon streusel muffins I'd left on the counter obviously had not been closed tightly enough, and the kittens had managed to figure out that if they knocked the container onto the floor, the lid would pop off and they could have a feast.

Unfortunately, they hadn't quite learned to use a broom yet, and pieces of muffin were ground up into my kitchen rug and all over their faces.

My cup of pens was knocked over, the neat pad of papers that I had beside my phone was no longer so tidy, and it appeared that the knitted hand towel I had hanging from the oven door was now one long piece of thread that did not resemble the towel it once was.

Gone was my night, quiet evening. Gone was the vision of soft jazz music in the background while I replied to Richard's email. Gone was the idea of curling up on the couch with a good book before bed.

I certainly didn't think I would spend the next hour cleaning up my kitchen.

Nor did I think that I would be too exhausted even to want to look at my computer once I had finished replanting my poor plants, winding up a ball of yarn, vacuuming my rugs, and then washing my floor to get rid of all the dirt marks.

Thankfully, I wasn't too tired to think about Rich, and I didn't want him to think I was ghosting him…so despite how tired I felt, I curled up on the couch, both kittens beside me sleeping and re-read his email.

I let my fingers fly as I replied, not giving myself the time to think about what my words.

Dear Rich, I still dream. Sometimes I'm dressed in a clown costume, other times, I'm locked in a room with chocolate molds that can talk, but most of the time, my dreams consist of me, the beach, and being content. Those are probably my favorite.
I don't run-and-jump anymore. Maybe I'm too chicken. Maybe I've been hurt too much in the past. Maybe…maybe I just don't have the right partner to jump with. But, maybe…just maybe…if you promise to hold on tight…
Come by for coffee. For the record, that mean cup of Joe you mentioned is the best coffee you've ever tasted, this side of the ocean, at least. It would be nice to catch up, to hear about this opportunity, and I'll even save you some dessert.
Who knows, maybe I'll even introduce you to the two new loves of my life…Wynne.
Ps. Attached is a photo of my babies. They're adorable when they sleep, and disasters when awake.

I took a photo of the kittens and added it to the email before I hit the send button. I closed the laptop with the full intention of going to sleep, but even in bed, my brain won't stop.

I opened a book but read the same page four times before I admitted defeat.

I checked my phone a dozen times, hoping, praying, needing a response...which was ridiculous because it was late, and the guy was probably fast asleep like I should have been.

Except, he wasn't.

Rich had written me back.

To my night owl;
Talking chocolate molds and clown costumes sound like nightmares. Being on the beach...now that sounds just about perfect. I hope you're not alone though. Or...maybe I do. Do you even dream about me? No...don't answer that. At least, not right now.

I'd love to come for coffee - sooner than later, if that's all right with you? Normally I'm a boring guy, work, sleep, ride my bike, or out in snowshoes, and rarely adventuring too far, but this weekend, I'm heading to some out-of-town friends. I'll be close enough that I could stop in Friday night and take some coffee to go?

I know it's short notice. If you have plans, we can arrange a time next week.

I really want to see you and will do anything to make it happen...Rich.

Any semblance of sleep flew out the window with his reply. Obviously, the answer to seeing him was a resounding yes, but the questions was when.

Friday night wouldn't work. I had that party and blind date.

Next week was too far away.

My brain wouldn't stop as I read through his email over and over. If he was close enough while visiting friends, did that mean he'd been in the area before but never stopped in? Or maybe he did, and Heather never told me?

What friends did he have in the area? It wasn't like I lived close to a highway - so how could he be close by?

Would that mean that he is coming here this weekend to see

me? Heather and Matt wouldn't be the 'friends' he talked about that had invited him to stay?

Heather wouldn't do that to me. Right?

I thought of my mother and this 'mystery' date, but not even my mother could pull this one off. My imagination was obviously working overtime and knowing there was no possible way of achieving sleep until this got resolved, I quickly called Heather, praying that she would answer and not Matt.

"Hey, what's up?" Heather greeted me as she answered the phone.

"Oh, good, I didn't wake you."

"Lucky for you, I'm just finishing off those desserts I told you I would make. What's up?"

"I have a question for you, and I'm hoping you'll be able to answer."

"Okay, ask away."

"You wouldn't, by chance, be involved with my mom in setting me up with this 'mystery date' for Friday night, would you?" I winced at the question, understanding how it sounded, but I needed to know.

"Why would I be involved in that? Your mom can play match-maker all by herself. She doesn't need my help." I heard the timer on her oven go off.

"Just a sec," she said, plopping the phone down on the counter. There was the background noise of her rummaging through drawers, then the slam of the oven door.

"Hey babe, ready for bed?" I heard Matt's voice in the distance and her shushing him.

"Wynne's on the phone," she said.

"Wynne? Go to bed. It's late." He almost yelled.

"Matt! She's on the phone, not deaf." There was a muffled noise, and then she whispered: "she's asking me about Friday."

"Friday? What? Oh....I'm out. I'm going to bed," he answered back, and then I could hear doors closing, and Heather was back on the phone.

"Sorry about that. Okay, what's this about your mom?"

"What's happening this weekend?" I might as well come right out with it and not beat about the bush.

"This weekend? Besides the party? I have no idea."

"Come on, Heather…" She was being too cagey, and I didn't believe her at all.

"I'm not in cahoots with your mom on anything, I promise."

I hummed and hawed. Did I believe her? I wasn't sure.

"If not my mother, what about Richard? He sent me another email and—"

She let out a very long sigh. "Wynne, I'm tired," she said, interrupting me. "I don't know what's going through your brain, but I can't keep up, okay? Night."

No warning. No goodbye. She just hung up.

I looked at the phone. I wasn't even given a chance to say good night. That wasn't like her at all. I either caught her at a bad time…or she knew more than she let on.

Something was off. Something was wrong. Something was happening around me, regarding me, and I was being left in the dark.

I didn't like that. Not one bit.

CHAPTER TWENTY-THREE

every girl needs to be pampered

Friday came too fast and I wasn't prepared.

Offering to throw this party had to have been one of the stupidest, most impulsive decisions I'd made in a long time.

Didn't matter that I regretted it since I offered.

Didn't matter that everyone and their pet stepped in to help me.

Didn't matter that, technically, I wasn't the one putting on this party anymore...I was still attached to it.

If ever I wished I were sick with a cold, it was now. Then I could stay home, and no one would think twice about it.

That morning, I'd woken up tasting chocolate and caramel. It was one of my favorite duos and, for one very specific reason.

When Richard and I were dating in college, we would often come back here on the weekends and visit my parents. Just outside of town is a little park, complete with its own stream.

One day Rich decided that he wanted to teach me how to skip rocks. We had just started to date, and the newness of everything was so unique and special. Before we arrived, we had stopped at the ice cream shop in town and bought a large sundae to split.

I loved chocolate, and he wanted caramel, so we combined the two flavors together. There was a little bench in front of the stream where we sat and ate our sundae together, and then Rich showed me how to skip rocks. I could still feel his arms around me, holding me close, guiding my hand in throwing the rock in just the right way onto the water.

I never learned how to make it skip. Mine would just plop into the water, while he would glide his rocks across the water with barely a ripple.

Last night, I had a dream about him. Go figure. Lately, that was all I was dreaming about…dreaming, daydreaming, journalling, praying…he consumed my thoughts and my heart.

But, in my dream, we were at that spot sharing that same sundae. Instead of skipping rocks, Rich declared his undying love to me. We were standing by a tree that was close to the water. My back was against him, and he held me in his arms. It was a comfortable feeling. As if this was the place that I was meant to be.

In my ear, Richard was professing his love, his commitment, and his desire for us to be together. It was such a sweet romantic dream.

Until my kittens decided it was time for me to wake up. One was at my ear licking it, and the other managed to find my toe at the end of the bed and decided it was a new toy.

That was not the way that I wanted to wake up.

Apparently, I had no choice because my phone started to go off.

"Good morning, sweetheart," my mother greeted me after I finally answered.

"That depends, Mom. Why are you calling me so early?" I mumbled. All I wanted to do was close my eyes and go back to la-la land.

"Wynne, dear. Wake up. I'm outside your door. It's not exactly warm out today. I have coffee and bagels if that will help."

That jolted me out of bed. I slid into my slippers, grabbed my big comfy bathrobe, and shuffled my way to the front door where my mother stood banging on it with her fist.

"Brrrr." The wind twisted around my ankles and slid its way up my bare legs. "It's like the North Pole out there," I said as I looked up and saw not only my mother but the Latte Ladies with her, all bundled up nicely against the chilly weather.

"Um...what's going on?" It was way too early for everyone to be here.

Mom pushed past me and led the way into the kitchen. I stood there, taking everyone's coats and scarves, and watched as they took their place around my table.

I dropped their coats on my couch in the living room and then joined them, thankful for the cup of coffee someone shoved in my hands.

It was a little too obvious I wasn't quite awake yet.

"I hope you don't mind us coming so early, but we have a lot to do and we needed an early start." Mom pulled out a chair and gestured for me to sit.

I looked around the room, feeling like I was missing something.

"I'm confused?" If I had my notebook, I could go over the itinerary for the day. "I sent out the timetable earlier this week, didn't I?" Please tell me I didn't forget to do that.

I breathed a sigh of relief as everyone nodded. "Okay, so... we'll meet up at the church around noon to start decorating. I'll be a t the church later this afternoon to start taking care of the food, and a few of you will be joining me to help."

Again with the nods.

"So, what am I missing?" I took a sip of my coffee, thankful the cobwebs were disappearing from my mind.

Tracey spoke up. "Wynne, you've had such a busy week that we all decided you needed a little pampering today. You have an appointment this morning at 9:30 at The Pampering Palace for a full morning of spa treatments."

"I...what? Are you...no--"

"Then," Tracey held up a finger to stop me from speaking. "Then at lunch a few of us are taking you on a shopping trip to pick out a stunning dress for tonight. Once we find that dress, you have an appointment back at The Pampering Palace for a makeover and a style. You are going to look like you walked out of a magazine by the time tonight comes around."

Everyone but me giggled. Did they not realize it was way too early in the morning for giggling?

The Pampering Palace was the only spa place in town. The last time I was in there was the morning of my wedding three years ago.

"I don't need a makeover, or a new dress or even a spa day," I grumbled.

"What woman doesn't want a spa day?" Mom asked. "Besides, we can't have your mystery date seeing you tonight looking like you just spent the week organizing the whole event. He needs to see you in the very best light, relaxed and stunning." There was a note of finality in Mom's voice, and a quick tightening of her gaze to tell me not to argue.

I decided to ignore that look.

"Mom, come on. This is all a little..." I searched for the right word, "too much, don't you think?" I looked to Tracey for backup, but she only shook her head at me.

"Why are you even arguing with me?" Mom asked. "Don't you worry about tonight, we ladies have it handled, and we don't want to see you there until later, do you hear me?" Her finger wagged in the air, and I was going to argue, I was absolutely going to argue, but a hand landed on my knee with a tight squeeze, and I realized any argument from me wouldn't have mattered.

"I'd really prefer if you canceled this date, Mom." The words came out as a whispered plea.

"Cancel? No, I won't do that. It's too late anyway. I know, I know," Mom said with an eye roll, "not to get my hopes up, but a mother can hope, can't she? I want grandbabies, Wynne and if it means setting you up on dates, then I'll do what I need to do."

Her lips thinned, and I couldn't tell if she was embarrassed or frustrated. Probably a little bit of both.

Grandbabies? She had to bring that up, didn't she?

I didn't want to get into this with the other ladies around, so I just sighed and kept quiet. I think she took that as my acceptance because she produced a huge smile and clapped her hands together in delight.

"Well, the past couple of days have literally flown by, it seems." I hesitated when I noticed the hopeful gazes in everyone's eyes. "Who could pass up a day of pampering and being made to feel like a princess?"

I felt somewhat resigned. Amongst the squeals of delight that I had accepted so easily, Judy whispered in my ear to enjoy the day stop worrying so much.

CHAPTER TWENTY-FOUR

feeling like a princess

Mom was right. Every woman deserved a day of pampering.

After hours of being treated like royalty, I began to feel like a princess amongst the scrubbing and pounding massages.

All this pampering could really get to a girl's head. It took a minute, but I told myself it was okay to enjoy the day.

And enjoy it, I did. I enjoyed the fresh smoothies, the warming beds, the pedicure, the manicure, and even the hot stone massage. Being pampered was a treat, and regardless of the reasons behind it, I enjoyed every moment of it.

At exactly noon, Heather and Tracey joined me on a shopping trip. Shopping with these two was an experience all on its own. Tracey relished the day with no kids, and Heather, well, Heather just loves to shop.

Me, I wasn't a shopper. Sure, I enjoyed it online, and when it involved finding items for the shop, but for myself? Give me yoga pants and hoodies…basically anything that spoke comfort.

Apparently the women had their own ideas on what kind of dress I needed for tonight and it took two exhausting hours of them forcing me to try on different styles before I found something we all agreed on.

It was an exotic black dress with embroidered island-colored flowers flowing on the hem. The skirt of this dress swirled around my legs as I spun around. It had a scooped neckline that included a scarf in the same exotic colors detailed on the skirt. The sleeves were three-quarter length with a small cuff.

I felt beautiful. I was beautiful.

We had just enough time to return to the Pampering Palace for the rest of my beauty treatment - the transformation that included a cut and makeup treatment.

I spent another two hours in that chair. I wasn't allowed to look in the mirror the whole time, being told to trust the process. The process involved too much effort, as far as I was concerned, and reminded me too much of my failed wedding day.

Whatever happened tonight didn't deserve all this commitment, but I went with it, mainly because I wasn't given a choice. Every time I grumbled, I'd get death stares from both Heather and Tracey and I felt guilty.

Why? I had no idea.

When it was time for the grand reveal, I saw the looks on my friends faces and figured something was wrong.

"What? What is it?" I twisted in the chair, needed to see what had gone so horribly wrong, but all I could do was sit and gasp at the face in the mirror.

My face.

"And there she is...the woman who has been hiding for the past three years..." Heather stood behind me and gave me a hug.

"I haven't been hiding." I heard the lie, even as I said it. I peeked over at Tracey, who looked just as surprised as I felt.

"Yes, you have been hiding, and you know it. And you shouldn't. I mean...girl, we always need a reminder of just how beautiful we are, inside and out."

I blushed. They were right. I hadn't felt this...stunning...since my wedding day, and for a plethora of reasons that I didn't want to acknowledge.

"It's crazy what the right cut and color can do for a woman."

The stylist said. "Your reactions, that's what I aim for with every treatment. Whomever you are seeing tonight, I sure hope he appreciates it."

"Oh, he'll appreciate it, especially once you're in your new dress. Speaking of which...we're running late." Tracey handed me my coat while Heather pushed me out the door.

I caught glimpses of myself by the reflection in the windows, but I didn't see the whole effect until I had my new dress on. WOW. I almost didn't recognize myself. My haircut was in a layered bob just below my chin, my eyes seemed accentuated and the colors used on my face were so natural yet bold.

I've never been a big fan of a lot of makeup – a little mascara here, some eyeliner there, and of course some lipstick for color, but that's about it. But I had to admit that I was amazed at how put together I looked.

Perhaps a little more effort on my part wouldn't hurt now and then.

I stepped out of my room and walked down the hallway. The looks on Heather and Tracey's faces said enough.

"Wow, Wynne. Stunning. Your date won't know what hit him!" Tracey exclaimed.

"Promise me something, girl?" asked Heather. "Promise me that you will just soak in everything tonight and not overthink, please?"

I smiled. That was easy.

"I promise." Right now, anything could happen to me and I would run with it.

If Brad Pitt were to enter the church tonight and ask me on a date, I would definitely run with it.

I glanced down at my watch and realized that it was after five. I had originally planned on being at the church by now to help with all the last-minute preparations.

"All right girlies, the coach awaits." I bundled up in my winter coat and prepared to leave.

Thank goodness the weather had decided to cooperate. Even

though it was wintertime, it was fairly mild out that night, despite all the snow that we had received the past week.

Some of the snowfall had melted away. Snowmen sagged in the front yards and some were barely even standing anymore. No need to shovel the walkway, in fact, you could probably have gone for a stroll with a warm sweater, scarf, and mittens that night if you'd felt so inclined.

Heather had Christmas music playing in her vehicle. With all the Christmas lights sparkling from the trees and homes, you could definitely feel the spirit of Christmas. As the girls dropped me off at the church and then pulled away to get themselves ready for the night, I decided to slowly walk up the walkway to the church.

With the warm breeze blowing, and snow on the ground, you could almost feel the magic in the air. I found myself whistling "Walking in a Winter Wonderland" and feeling at peace within my heart. I couldn't stop myself from silently praising God for all His goodness in my life.

I spread out my arms and did a little twirl on the sidewalk. With all the beauty surrounding me, I almost felt like God had created this night with me in mind.

"Thank you, Father," I whispered, "for this wonderful blessing.

As I stepped through the door of the church, I gasped. The sight before me was that of an indoor winter palace. The ladies had done such an amazing job.

The moment you walked into the church you felt like you had been transported to a winter getaway. A Christmas tree stood alone in the corner, sparkling with lights and cranberries gracing the tree. There was a small table with candles glowing and a beautifully decorated book for guests to sign and write precious words of wisdom for the couple to treasure for years to come.

A little bench stood beside the tree for women to sit and exchange their boots for shoes if they desired, and one of the youths of the church was standing beside the coat rack, offering to hang coats for those just walking in.

The lights had been turned down low so the only glow was from the Christmas lights on the ceiling as well as the tree, and the dozen candles that were blazing throughout the room.

To reach the downstairs you walked down a winding staircase. Normally the walls of the staircase were decorated with posters for Children's Church and various mission projects that the Sunday classes had taken on. That night though, these posters had been taken down and replaced with various printed frames portraying elegance and delicacy.

One picture was a snowflake, another of an outdoor winter scene. There was a large picture in the middle with white embossed paper and a gold ribbon as the only source of decoration on that frame.

Winding their way down the stairs were even more soft white Christmas lights. When you reached downstairs, currently the door was closed, obstructing the view of the inside. Before the closed door was another Christmas tree, decorated with white lights and gold ribbon. Simple, yet elegant in appearance.

When I opened the door the signs of busyness excited me.

Various ladies from the church were there creating the final touches to the décor in the room. When I mentioned that I wanted elegant, that is exactly what I received.

I stopped just inside the door and took a good look around the room. My mom was holding court over in the far corner. From what I could see, she was in charge here – *good job, Mom*. I gave her a quick thumbs up.

All around the room were round tables that would each seat between six to eight people. They were arranged in a circular design with a main round table in the middle.

Stacey loved pink and wanted it incorporated into the design for the night. Since Stacey and Jude would be sitting at the middle table, the underlining skirt was a deep rose color with a shorter gold color cloth on top. Their chargers were gold with white plates rimmed with a bold black stripe. For the centerpiece, there was a vase filled with floating candles and pink sparkles. Arranged around the vase were pink-coloured votives. Just perfect.

As you walked into the room, beside the door was another Christmas tree decorated with white sparkling lights and white and pink ribbon and strings. Christmas lights were strung on the ceiling as well as thick tube-like lights outlined the room on the floor. Soft instrumental music played in the background. The women were adding the final touches to each table, and I could see others in the kitchen arranging various dishes of desserts.

A long table against one wall was decorated in pink and gold. I assumed this would be the table for the desserts and punch. Beside the tree was a table in the same colors with wrapped gifts already on top.

As I stood there Judy and Pastor Joy from the Latte Ladies approached to give me hugs. They looked like they were on their way out.

"Wynne, you look amazing. A fairytale princess come true," gushed Pastor Joy while admiring my dress.

"Being pampered suits you. You're beautiful," admired Judy.

"Thanks. I had so much fun, thank you so much for doing this for me." I gave each lady a hug. "This place looks fantastic and is so much more than I could have imagined."

"You have your mother to thank for that. She made sure that all your ideas were workable and that we all helped to create this dream," Pastor Joy informed me.

"Now we have to be off and get ready ourselves. Have fun, and we'll see you soon." Judy walked out the door.

After they left, I walked over to my mom and gave her a hug.

"Thank you so much, Mom. This is perfect." I was still amazed at how it all had come together.

"This is an important night, Wynne, I just wanted to make it perfect for you." Mom hugged me back, and I could see tears in her eyes.

168

"You look so beautiful," Mom cried as she gazed at me.

"Why is it so shocking to everyone?" I asked her. The reaction of everyone so far was leaving me with a weird feeling. Did I normally not look good, so that when I did dress up, the change was so startling that everyone noticed?

My mom reached up and patted my cheeks.

"Honey, your whole focus has been so much on your business and your home that you have forgotten to focus on yourself. So yes, the change in you tonight is so evident that everyone will notice. Don't be ashamed, just reach out and grab onto life the way God wants you to."

I smiled at her and knew that I had a twinkle in my eyes.

"I plan to, Mom, I plan to."

"Good," she replied. "Now go and grab an apron and help out in the kitchen. Make sure it's a full apron though; I don't want you to get your dress dirty. If you had listened to me in the first place, this wouldn't even be an issue." She scooted me towards the kitchen.

"Mom, if I had listened to you, then I would still be at home getting ready while you were here directing. Nope. It's time for you to go home now and get ready. Dad promised me he would come tonight." I took the clipboard that she was holding from her hand and walked her to the door.

With only an hour left before everyone would arrive, I made a quick sweep of the list my mom had created to see what else needed to be done. Noticing that everything had been checked off, I headed into the kitchen to see how I could help there. The moment I walked in Joan handed me an apron to put on. I just laughed and told her all mothers think alike.

"No, honey, this is a woman thing, not a mother thing. What woman in her right mind would want to get all messy after she has just spent a day of pampering and looks absolutely gorgeous?" she asked me with a southern twang to her voice.

I laughed as I worked on a tray of goodies.

CHAPTER TWENTY-FIVE

the party

The party was a success from the moment it started.

Jude and Stacey arrived a few minutes early, I made sure I was at the front door to greet them.

Jude made the average male comment. "Very nice," he said while shrugging off his jacket and taking Stacey's wrap.

Thankfully, Stacey had a completely different reaction. The moment she walked into the front entrance, she was enthralled. "Oh, Wynne. This is amazing. It's gorgeous," she gushed.

"Just wait until you see the downstairs," I warned her.

"Oh, I can't wait. Come on, Jude," she cried as she tugged at his hand.

I followed them down the stairs and soaked in all the comments Stacey made on her way down. Although I hadn't personally created the atmosphere here tonight, I felt so proud of those who had.

Just as we reached the bottom of the stairs, I called to Jude and asked him to wait. I gave Stacey a moment to gather her thoughts. I wanted to share something that was in my heart with them, but I didn't want Stacey to be so completely focused on the decorations that she lost what I had to say.

"Jude, tonight is such a special night for you and Stacey. There were so many ladies that came today to help make this whole night a possibility. There will be time tonight for you both to have a few words. Could you make sure that you give them all the credit and not me?" I asked him.

If I remembered correctly, Jude had a habit of not thinking before speaking, and I wanted to make sure that he didn't end up sticking both feet in his mouth tonight.

"Of course, Wynne. I know how much you hate having the spotlight on yourself. Don't worry. Even though I know you were the mastermind behind tonight, I'll place all the glory on the others," Jude informed me.

"No, that's not what I meant. Jude, Stacey, the moment I made the decision to throw this party for you, I had so many people rally around me, concerned that I was doing this for all the wrong reasons. They decided, all on their own, I might add, to throw this party for you instead – as a group. All the ladies who helped to raise you in this church are the ones you should be thanking tonight." I wanted to make sure that they understood who really deserved the attention.

Stacey took hold of my hands. "Wynne, we completely understand. This will be a night where we will always remember that this church showered love upon us." Stacey confirmed exactly what I was hoping to hear.

"Thank you, Stacey. This night is for you guys, and I hope you'll enjoy it. I am so happy for you both." I told them as I opened the door to the main room.

Inside, the majority of those who were coming had already shown up. Everyone waited for the guests of honor to arrive.

Pastor Joy offered to host the evening, leaving me with barely anything to do. Once I walked the newly engaged couple into the room, I was free to melt into the crowd and wait for my mystery date to arrive.

The moment Jude and Stacey walked into the room, everyone clapped. I hung back a little bit, giving the couple enough time to walk into the room and mingle.

I guess I waited too long because just as I was about to enter, Heather walked out the door searching for me.

"What are you doing out here by yourself? Waiting for your date?" She reached for my hand.

"No. I'm sure my mom will find me when he arrives. I was just giving them some time to get in before I followed them." In all honesty, I hadn't thought about my mystery date too much tonight. I thought I would leave the introductions up to my mom whenever he decided to arrive.

"Well, come on then. You don't want people to wonder where you are, do you?"

"I hope you saved me a seat." We wove our way through the crowd.

"Of course, I saved you a seat. I'm offended. What kind of friend would I be to leave you on your own with a mystery date?"

"Hmm, that is true. You'll need to grill him and decide if he's good enough or not," I teased as we found our seats.

"You know her too well," confirmed Matt, overhearing our conversation.

Heather just grinned, not at all embarrassed that we had figured out her true intentions.

"So where is this mystery man?" Matt asked.

"I figure there are two reasons why he's not here yet. One, my mother gave him her famous directions, and he's now on the other side of town completely lost, or two, his sanity returned, and he realized what a horrible idea this was," I said, smiling.

Matt and Heather laughed. My mother's sense of direction was famous around here. You only have to experience getting lost once before you figure out that the opposite way from what she told you was the right way.

My childhood was all about getting lost on road trips because Mom couldn't read the map properly. When my mom tells you to turn left, you turn right. When she tells you that it's just down the road a bit, be prepared for a long drive.

"I would bank on the fact that he got turned around," Matt

told me. "Any guy who would turn down a date with you tonight needs to be in a mental hospital."

"Doesn't she look fantastic tonight?" Heather reiterated for the millionth time tonight. I knew she was just trying to boost my self-esteem, but enough already.

"All right, all right, enough, please. It's embarrassing," I said in mock anger.

"Just soak it up, will you? No woman in her right mind would deny a compliment when she deserves it," Heather said.

I was beginning to feel a bit antsy, and I needed to move around.

"I'm not denying it, Heather. I just don't need to hear it anymore." I walked away from her.

CHAPTER TWENTY-SIX
true love

About an hour into the party, I was beginning to feel like I had been stood up.

By now, all the guests had arrived, and the majority of the food had been eaten. Stacey was in the middle of opening the numerous gifts that they received while Jude sat there fiddling with his drink and looking completely bored. I was still feeling quite antsy and was constantly moving around.

I found myself continually watching the door.

I walked over to my parent's table.

"Now be patient, dear. I know he's a little late but will be here." Mom patted my hand. What was with her patting my hand? Not only was I feeling a bit antsy, but I was also starting to feel a bit grumpy.

"Mom, he's an hour late. It's quite obvious that he won't be coming, whoever he is. Thanks for the thought, though. I do appreciate it."

"He'll be here, honey," My dad interjected.

"Well, I'm glad that you both feel positive about this. I don't even know the guy, but if he has enough bad manners to not show up on a date, then I'm fairly certain that I don't want to waste my time getting to know him," I reasoned.

"Be patient, dear. Now, why don't you go grab your mother a fresh cup of punch and something to munch on? Preferably chocolate if there is any left," she asked me, or rather, told me.

There wasn't much of a selection left, even though the night was only half over. Making a mental note to go into the kitchen to see if there were any plates to bring out, I filled my mom's punch glass and placed it on the table while I glanced through the remaining selections of dessert.

I chose a piece of chocolate brownie and a pecan tart for my mom and was just about to take the final piece of cheesecake for myself when from behind me, I could hear my name being called.

I turned, and my plate slipped from my hand.

There, standing before me, was my date.

My body shook as I stood there in complete shock and could not form a single thought, let alone a word.

He just stood there. There was a gentle smile on his face and a twinkle in his eye.

I wanted to kiss him.

All I could do was stare.

"This is where you are supposed to say hello," he said softly.

Hello? Hello? How in the world could I even imagine saying 'hello' when I was finding it difficult to comprehend the very fact that he was standing before me with a bouquet of roses in his hand and a smile on his face?

"Okay, well, how about 'am I dreaming' if you can't say hello," he continued. He had one of those earth-shattering lazy smiles on his face. I could tell he loved my reaction.

My smile mirrored his.

"Am I dreaming?" I asked him teasingly. Everything else had faded into the background. The only person in my reality at that moment was the one standing before me.

"Richard?" I asked hesitantly. I felt in my heart I knew the answer of why he was here, but I still needed to ask. "Why are you here?"

Richard stepped closer. His eyes—promised something I couldn't dare to dream.

"I've come to make your dreams come true," he whispered to me softly.

I was lost in the moment. Everything in my heart screamed 'YES', and I felt my body respond in the same manner.

"You are my dream come true," I whispered back to him as I closed the space between us. I raised my hands to his face. I needed to physically touch him in order to convince myself that he was really here and not just a dream.

I closed my eyes when my hand rested on his face. He whispered my name. I wanted, no, I needed to soak in this moment, a moment that was real and not just a dream.

I opened my eyes and smiled.

"Hi," I whispered.

With that, Rich's eyes lit up, and he laughed.

I reached out my hand toward him. He slowly brought his hand forward, a questioning look on his face.

"I'm Wynne," I introduced myself. "You must be my mystery date," I said to him with laughter in my voice.

It took Rich a moment to grasp what I was doing, but once he realized that we had an audience, he slowly shook my hand.

"Wynne, what a beautiful name for such a beautiful lady," he began. "My name is Rich, and I'm your mystery man. I hope you don't mind that I brought you some roses." He handed me the beautiful bouquet.

While our hands were intertwined together, my mother walked over to my side, a beaming smile on her face. Then came Heather and Matt. The boys shook hands before Heather turned to me with a smile on her face.

"Do you have any idea how difficult this was to keep a secret?" she asked me.

"You knew," I accused her while wagging my finger in her face. "How could you know about this and not tell me?"

"You have no idea how hard it was for her, Wynne." Matt placed his arms around his wife.

"Seriously, you have no idea," Heather agreed while she nestled in his arms.

"There were so many times I had to stop from even hinting at what was happening. Gah. I thought for sure I'd slip up."

I wasn't about to let them all off that easily.

"So what about the time we went out to Mama Rose's for dinner? If it was such a secret, why did you tell me you had been in touch with Rich?" I demanded.

Richard answered before Heather had the chance to.

"I was the one who asked her to do that," he admitted to me. "I wanted you to start thinking about having me back in your life, and I knew Heather was the perfect person to help make that happen," he told me.

My mother turned to me.

"Honey, you're not upset with us, are you?" she asked.

"How exactly do you fit into this picture, Mom?" I responded in turn with a question of my own.

Again Richard was the one to provide the answer.

"After Heather gave me the heads up that you hadn't forgotten about me, I decided to get in touch with your mom and see if she could help me."

"Such perfect timing," my mother jumped in. "He called right after Nancy informed me about tonight's party, and you know me, I got the great idea of him coming tonight as your guest."

"Hmm, so basically, you all knew about this and just left me in the dark." I felt hurt that they would keep this from me, but also a bit of happiness that they would do this for me.

At that moment, when everyone was silent, trying to figure out a way to get out of the situation they placed themselves in, Tracey walked up.

"You made it," Tracey loudly exclaimed while she threw her arms around Rich and gave him a hug.

This captured the attention of all the others in the room that hadn't previously noticed us.

Richard placed his hands on Tracey's shoulders and stood back from her.

"Look at you," he said. "Mother of three, a pastor's wife, and you're as lovely as ever." Rich complimented her while Pastor Mike, her husband, walked over.

"Hey, man. Long time no see," greeted Mike warmly. Richard and Mike had become friends while we were all together in school.

I was starting to feel a bit awkward just standing there while being ignored by one set of friends and being watched by those still seated at their tables around the room.

"Ahem," I called out. "I do believe that this is my mystery date," I pouted.

"Would you be greatly offended if I whisked you away tonight, Wynne?" Rich asked.

"Well, I really should stick around to help clean up," I said hesitantly.

"Nonsense." My mother spoke up, just as I was hoping she would. "You kids go on. Just leave the cleanup to me." She pushed me towards Richard.

Just as Rich reached out to grasp my hand, Mike spoke up.

"We'll leave the door unlocked for you, Rich."

I looked up at Rich with a question in my eyes. "So they are the friends?"

"I thought for sure I'd said too much in that email. I guess not, huh?"

I couldn't keep the smile off my face. Tracey hugged me and whispered in my ear.

"Make your dreams become reality."

I closed my eyes, took a deep breath, and walked with Richard towards the door. When I had enough nerve, I glanced up at him, only to find him smiling down at me.

"I am so glad that you are really here," I said.

"I've waited a long time to hear you say that." His eyes sparkled.

We had just finished walking through the doorway and were about to walk up the stairs when we heard someone walking quickly behind us.

CHAPTER TWENTY-SEVEN

second chances

I t was Jude, with an odd look in his eyes, almost as if he knew immediately that this was the man who claimed my heart so long ago.

Richard kept his gaze on Jude as he walked towards us. I could feel a slight tightening of his hand as he held mine.

On the other hand, Jude's shoulders seemed stooped as he stood there. The tension between the two men was quickly mounting.

"Jude, I'd like you to meet Richard. Richard, this is Jude. Tonight's party is to celebrate his new engagement with the beautiful lady standing right behind him," I nervously introduced the two men and saw Stacey standing in the background, watching the exchange.

Both of the men nodded their heads at each other while they shook hands.

Stacey walked up to Jude and placed her arm around his waist.

Richard then placed his arm around my shoulders.

"Well," I said, trying to break the tension. "I hope you don't mind that I am leaving early," I said to Stacey.

"Not at all," she replied with a sweet smile. "Thank you so much for everything."

I glanced over at Jude and gave him a smile. I watched him as his gaze went from me to Richard and then back to me again.

"Nice meeting you, Jude," Richard said. "Congratulations, and I pray that you find happiness together."

"Goodnight," I called out as Rich, and I began to walk up the stairs.

"So that was the man I thought had taken you away from me," Richard said quietly as we walked up.

"That was the man who refused to become second best," I squeezed his hand.

"Hmmm," was all he said, helping me into my jacket.

Richard walked me down the walkway. When we were halfway down, he stopped and lifted his head to the sky.

"It's such a beautiful night, a night of new beginnings," I said to him.

The tenderness in his eyes stole my breath.

"What are you thinking?" I asked him.

He stood there silently for a moment as we stared into each other's eyes.

"I was just thanking God that He is the God of second chances."

There was nothing that I could say to that. It was the perfect description of what was beginning to happen between us.

I turned to face him. I couldn't help but show my emotions to him. Tears welled up. He gently brought me to him in a gentle hug. It felt so good to be held in his arms. I took a deep breath, breathing in the very essence of him. He placed his cheek against the top of my head.

"Do you feel it?" he whispered as I stood there in his arms.

"The peace?" I asked him.

"Knowing that this is the place where you belong, in my arms," he responded.

I shivered. Thinking I was cold, Rich gently withdrew from the hug and led me toward his vehicle.

After climbing into his black Ford Escape, Richard quickly put the heater on, and we sat there waiting for the vehicle to warm up.

"I wasn't cold, you know," I said to him.

"No?"

I blushed and glanced out the window, trying to gather my thoughts.

"So, since this is officially classified as a date … do you have any ideas of what we should do tonight?" I asked him.

"Hmm, I have some thoughts," he responded with the exact same look in his eyes that I knew I had in mine.

"Can I ask what they are?" I ventured.

He chuckled.

"I had originally thought of taking you to the park where we used to skip rocks, but since it's the middle of winter, that won't do. Then I thought of going to a coffee shop where we could sit and chat, but then I realized that if I was to be honest, I just want to spend some time with you alone, not surrounded by other people."

"Would you consider two kittens an invasion of privacy?" I asked him, forming a plan in my head.

"Would these kittens insist on sharing some of the pasta and dessert I picked up from Mama Rose?" he asked me with a smile.

"You went to Mama Rose's already?" I squinted.

"Why do you think it took me so long to get here tonight? She recognized me the moment I walked in and held me hostage for over an hour before allowing me to leave with enough food to feed an army." He held his hands up in mock surrender.

Knowing Mama Rose, I could picture this clearly in my mind. That is exactly what she would do, not caring that she was holding him up or that I would be impatiently waiting for him at the church tonight.

Of course, I had no idea he was my mystery date, but still.

I giggled.

"So what did she make you leave with? Please tell me there is a piece of cheesecake in there," I begged him.

"A piece? Oh, come on, Wynne. There's a whole cake just for us, including some delicious pasta, garlic bread, and salad. She even placed an extra surprise in the bag, one she knew you would like," he told me with a hint of suspense in his voice.

"Oh, let me guess. Knowing Mama Rose, she probably placed some candles in the bag to add to the romance," I suggested.

Rich just winked at me as he drove out of the church parking lot.

I gave him directions to my house, feeling a bit nervous about him coming in. I hadn't had time to clean up my house yet, and the mess in the kitchen from this morning when the ladies brought breakfast over to the house was still there.

When we pulled up in front of my home, there were little jars filled with candles lining the sidewalk up to my door. Richard smiled and shrugged his shoulder as he stepped out of his door to walk around the vehicle to open my door.

"Don't ask," he said, "just enjoy."

I was rapidly trying to think of who would have come over to do this when Richard reached into his pocket and pulled out a key. When he inserted that key into the door to unlock it, I was about to ask him where he got the key when he placed his finger on my lips and said, "shush."

The moment I walked into my front hallway, I saw that someone had already thought ahead and prepared my home for our romantic date.

My house was not only spotless, but there was a soft glow coming from the living room, and dining room, and I could even see the soft flickering of candlelight coming from the kitchen.

I could hear the kittens quietly meowing and assumed that whoever had come over tonight also placed the kittens in my bedroom.

Taking off our coats and shoes, Richard took my hand and led me through my living room and into the dining room. The table had already been set with my grandmother's china, candles lit and even more flowers filled the room than the bouquet that I held in my hands.

"This is beautiful," I said as I took in all the candles and flowers.

"Why don't you place those flowers in a vase? The dinner has been placed in the oven on low to keep it warm," he informed me.

I smiled at him and felt so contented.

"How did you do all this?" I asked him as I walked over and gave him a hug.

"Tracey and Mike were the ones to do this. They came over here and met me as I brought the food. Tracey placed our meal in the oven to keep warm, set the table, and even placed all the candles on your walkway. Mike helped me to light all the candles, and then just before we left, Tracey locked your kittens in your room. I hope you don't mind?" he asked me somewhat hesitantly.

"Not at all," I responded, feeling somewhat surprised. How like Tracey to do this. I'd have to make sure to thank her properly later.

We spent the majority of our time at the table catching up on little things. I think we both decided to just go with the moment, to just enjoy what is going on for right now.

After enjoying a delicious meal, being surrounded by candle-light, and feeling like I was living in a dream, I offered to make some coffee and invited Richard to sit in the living room.

It had been such a long time, and while it would have been so easy to allow the romance of the evening to sweep us away, it was time to touch the ground, even for a moment, and talk about what was happening.

There was a little bit of an awkward moment that developed. Rich decided to be the first to breach the moment.

"So that was Jude," he said. A moot point since I had intro-duced him earlier that evening, but it was the only way to bring up the subject neither one of us really wanted to discuss. At least I knew I definitely didn't want to discuss it. I'd much rather sink into his arms and tell him about the dreams I had been having the past year or so.

"That was Jude," I responded.

"For three years, I thought you were off limits, a married woman. Do you know that I came to see you the day you got married, or at least the day I thought you were to be married?" he asked me.

I sat up straight.

"I had no idea, Rich. Where were you? What happened?" I asked him. A part of my heart sank.

"From the day you walked away from me, Wynne, I couldn't stop thinking about you. I prayed for you continually. I really believed that you were the woman that God created to make me complete. I knew you needed some time, so I gave you time. After two years, I couldn't take it anymore. I had it all planned. I would buy you roses; declare my undying love to you, and we would live happily ever after. I felt so good about it. I arrived in town and stopped at the florist to buy you roses. When I walked into the store, you should have seen the bouquets being arranged. The lady was on the phone, so I found a bouquet that I liked and walked up to the counter. I could hear the woman talking about a wedding that was to start in an hour. I thought I heard your name, but I wasn't sure. Then I looked down, and there on the counter was your wedding invitation. I thought for sure I read it wrong, but when I asked the florist she seemed so happy for you. I was in shock, Wynne. I couldn't believe it." Richard reached out and grabbed the coffee I'd made earlier.

I remained silent, knowing that he needed to finish.

"I rushed over to the church, and I saw the parking lot full of vehicles and people walking around all dressed up. I walked into the church and saw your guest book with your names. My heart broke into a million little pieces. I think that was the lowest point of my life. Up until then, I had always felt so sure that you were the perfect woman for me, and that God would eventually bring us together. On that day all my dreams were destroyed," Rich whispered.

We were both silently crying, and I reached over and grabbed his hand. He began to rub my hand with his thumb. A very comforting feeling.

"I went home and decided to start a new life. I felt betrayed by God, and it took me a long time to deal with that. Forgiving God is very hard; I found that out the hard way. But forgiving ourselves for allowing our hearts to lose trust in God is even harder. Every once in a while, I would talk to Tracey and Mike, but after that day, I made them promise never to mention your name to me. I had to completely cut you off from my life. But that never works, does it? Do you have any idea what it is like to feel guilty for finding your thoughts automatically dwell on a woman you thought was married for the past three years?" he asked me in anguish. My heart was breaking while listening to his story.

"Oh Rich. I'm so sorry." That was barely enough, but I couldn't say anything else.

"Wynne, don't ever apologize. If I hadn't been stubborn, I would have found out the truth a long time ago," he told me with a sigh.

"So, how did you find out that I never was married?" I asked him.

"Heather," he responded. "I ran into her one day, quite by accident, and before I could stop myself, I found myself asking her about you. You wouldn't believe the shock I felt when she told me that you had started a store with her and her husband and that you were still single," he confessed.

"Believe me, Richard, when I tell you that I can imagine," I told him, remembering how I felt when Heather told me that he wasn't married like I thought he must have been.

"Well," he said. "It was finding out that you were still single, and that you, in fact, never did get married that made me start to believe that my dreams weren't destroyed, that there was still some hope. The rest you heard tonight at the church," he confessed to me, looking somewhat sheepish.

I breathed a deep sigh and then smiled.

"Rich, I couldn't get married that day. Jude always knew that you held a large part of my heart, and that he would always be second best. Probably at the same time that you came to the church, Jude came into the room where I was and asked me if I could ever give him my whole heart. When I told him that I would never be able to do that, we both decided that it wouldn't be right to settle for second best. You were the only man who has ever or will ever own my heart, Richard," I softly told him. I waited breathlessly for his response.

"Tell me about your dreams, Wynne," Richard asked me.

So for the next hour, I poured out my heart and shared my dreams. It was the perfect evening.

Realizing how late it was becoming, we made plans to spend the following day together. Now that the thought of a future was before us, we wanted to spend as much time together as we could.

I walked Richard to the doorway. We both stood there together and stared into each other's eyes. Richard pulled me closer to him and held me against his heart. I could hear the rhythm of his heart beating.

I gazed into his eyes. I thought he was going to kiss me, but instead, he placed a finger against my lips.

"There is something between us that has never gone away, and it never will. It is a gift from God that we have to accept. I love you. I have always loved you, and I always will love you. I want to ask you a question that I want you to pray about. Please don't answer me now, just think about it. I don't want to live another day without you in my life. I want you to be the other half of me. I need you to complete me. Please, Wynne, become my wife and fill that empty space in my heart that was created just for you." Richard pleaded with me with love shining through his eyes.

Before I could even answer him, he lowered his mouth and kissed me.

It was the type of kiss that made all those kisses in my dreams fade away. It was even better than my dreams. This kiss spoke of love, commitment, and promise.

Tears began to fill my eyes and fall down my face. Richard gently kissed those tears away and then whispered in my ear.

"Sweet dreams, my darling."

the proposal

6 Months Later

We were seated on the bench by the tree sharing a sundae together. He was eating all the caramel sauce while I was digging for the hot fudge. We had just finished doing our devotions together, a habit we developed after the night of our mystery date. Whether we were on-line together, on the phone or in person, we would do daily devotions that only helped to strengthen our relationship.

Rich had come up for the weekend. School semester was over and he had given his resignation to the school. This was his first weekend school free, and he wanted to enjoy it to the fullest.

With the warm weather upon us we decided to head to the park, our favorite place, and enjoy the sunshine. Of course we had to share a sundae.

The past six months have been wonderful. Richard and I have become so close to each other. We have redefined our relationship by getting to know each other all over again. So many things happened within the five-year period that shaped who we have become. It has been fun though discovering each other's little quirks.

While Richard had plans to only relax and enjoy this weekend, I had decided to rock his boat a little bit. Six months ago he asked me a question he wouldn't let me answer. It had never come up since then in words, but the thoughts and promise had always lingered between us.

With only half of the sundae left, I turned to Richard and gave him a kiss. He tasted like caramel and ice cream. Deliciously sweet and tempting.

"Richard," I began. "You asked me a question six months ago that you wouldn't let me answer at the time."

Licking some caramel sauce off of his plastic spoon, he grinned. "I did?" he asked me somewhat playfully.

I swatted him on the arm.

"You did," I answered. "I have an answer for you, but I think you need to ask me again," I told him with a little bit of prima donna attitude to my voice.

Rich had this mischievous look enter in his eyes when he answered me.

"Hmmm," he said thoughtfully. "I think you might need to refresh my memory some. Six months is a long time to remember something." He smiled.

I gave a playful smile and sighed.

"The question," I began, "was, will you marry me?"

"I will," he responded with a huge smile on his face.

I laughed.

"No. You are supposed to ask me that question," I protested.

"I don't understand, Wynne. You just proposed, I accepted, so now why do I have to ask you?" He took another bite of our sundae.

"Richard Carradine, don't you play games with me."

"Oh honey, I'm not playing games. You proposed, I accepted, and now our sundae is melting. Hurry up and eat your part before it's all gone." He plunged his spoon back into the ice cream.

Feeling somewhat flustered, I did as he suggested, not

thinking twice about it. I made sure I dug to the bottom where the gooey hot fudge had melted. Bringing the spoon to my mouth, I let it slide into my mouth and as I bit down, something hard hit my teeth.

Pulling the spoon from my mouth, I saw something round and shiny amongst the spoonful of ice cream that was still left on the spoon.

"Rich, what is this?" I asked him as a huge smile lit his face.

"Well, that my dear, looks to me like it's a ring to go along with your proposal," he said to me in a teasing voice.

"Ah, but is the ring for me or for you?" I asked him with a smile.

"We'll just have to see, now won't we?" He took the ring off of the spoon and wiped it off with a napkin.

There in the napkin was a beautiful gold ring holding the largest solitary diamond I had ever seen.

Getting down on his knees, Richard reached for my hand and slowly placed the ring on my finger.

"Wynne, will you fulfill my life long dream of becoming your husband? Will you fill that place in my heart completely that belongs to you? Will you become my wife?" Richard asked me with love shining in his eyes.

I leaned down and kissed him. It was a kiss full of love and happiness, promises and dreams come true.

"I love you, Richard Carradine, and would love to spend the rest of my life making all your dreams come true," I answered him with a smile.

Who said dreams never come true?

dear reader...

This book. This crazy, ridiculous, sweet women's fiction with romantic elements, book…was the very first book I'd ever written.

Here's how it came to be:

I married a pastor and we moved all over the country. We had three small daughters and despite having a Bachelor of Theology behind me, I wasn't happy, content, satisfied.

I was more than the titles in my life. I was more than a pastor, more than a pastor's wife, more than a young mother, or wife, or daughter, or friend, or confident, or baker…I was more than all that.

I searched everywhere to figure out the piece of me that was missing. I joined online 'forums' where I met so many wonderful women who encouraged me to find myself, to give myself permission to discover 'me' again.

It wasn't until we were living in Alberta, Canada, where I worked in an office, that I decided to give 'myself' a chance. My husband heard about a publishing contract and reminded me that I always wanted to write books.

So, while at work (yes, I know…I should have been working, not writing), I wrote this story. It took me six months. I had absolutely NO idea what I was doing - never took a writing class, didn't know there were things called 'writing groups' out there...I didn't even know how to plot out a story properly.

But that didn't matter. I wrote this story about a woman who loved chocolate. I always wanted to have my own chocolate shop - so why not write about one? I'm a hopeless romantic who believes in love...so why not add that in?

I wrote this book in 2005 and submitted it (without knowing it needed editing) to the publisher and wouldn't you know it...I won! The editors did their magic, but then suggested I learn my craft, that if I wanted this to be a career, I needed to be serious about learning how to write - and boy, how right they were!

Looking back...I can't tell you how many times I wish I could rewrite this story. Plot it out properly. Go deeper with the relationships. Add the romance in sooner. Do this story real justice...

But then this story wouldn't be the same story, would it?

This book has gone through a few changes. At first, it was titled 'Once Upon A Dream' - because that's what this story was - a dream for me. When I received the rights back, I changed the cover and retitled it to 'Chocolate Reality'. Now, years later, I'm recovering it again and giving it the real title I think it deserves - Second Chances at the Chocolate Blessings Cafe.

This story was the one that started it all. From 2005 to 2010, it took me another 5 years to learn the 'craft of writing'. I wrote a few romances, had them published with some small presses, but it wasn't until 2011 that I decided to write what was truly in my heart.

Yes, I love and believe in romance. But the stories I wanted to tell were about the mother's heart. I still love telling those stories...but I find as I age, as the stages in my life as a mother, woman, wife, evolve, so does my storytelling and the direction I take.

Who knew I'd start off in inspirational romance, and all these years later, I'd have written in multiple genres, from romance to women's fiction to suspense and even psychological thrillers. What a journey. What an adventure!

I can't wait to see what the future holds. I'm excited about the direction I'm taking in my writing, in the stories I want to share. Looking back, I see where I've grown and where I need to continue to grow.

Thank you for joining me on this journey, for coming on this adventure with me. And thank you for not judging me too harshly after reading this book...we all have to start somewhere, right?

Xoxo,

Steena Holmes

other sweet reads you may enjoy...

The Promise of Christmas:

For the past two years, Ashley Tanner has been trying to keep her promise to revitalize the small mountain town of Innsbruck, but it's starting to look like she's failing as mayor, and failure is never an option for her.

HALFWAY SERIES:

Halfway to Nowhere:

Nikki Landon walked away from her small town, Halfway, Montana, ten years ago, with no intentions of setting foot there again. But, when her mother dies unexpectedly, Nikki has no choice but to return, and this time with a secret she's been hiding.

Halfway in Between:

Secrets in a small town have a way of getting out, and if Melissa and Nikki aren't careful, this is one secret that could destroy everything.

Halfway to Christmas:

A lot has happened in Halfway, and this year the holidays are set to take on a whole new meaning.

LOVE AT THE CHOCOLATE SHOP SERIES:

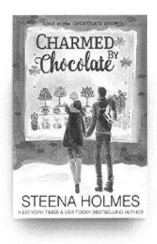

Book 6: CHARMED BY CHOCOLATE

After a mishap on a hit reality show called Charming, where she earns the name "Lonely Leah", she returns to Marietta to hide, never once dreaming she may find love back home.

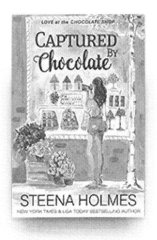

Book 11: CAPTURED BY CHOCOLATE

Radio DJ Dylan Morgan enjoys small-town life in Marietta. Unlike his longtime girlfriend and globetrotting photojournalist Casey Michaels, he's never been tempted to spread his wings.

Until an east coast job offer at a major radio station catches his eye. He considers taking the position, but then Casey calls...

She's coming home.

by steena holmes

If you enjoyed this story, you might enjoy:

Here's a *free read, just for signing up for my mailing list*

https://www.steenaholmes.com/newsletter-sign-up/

secret info on steena...

Here's some other fun things about me I bet you didn't know (want to ask me a question...find me on FB and I'll answer):

- I'm afraid of heights
  - Christmas is my favorite season
  - I'm a travelholic
  - spiders/bugs/bees... yep, afraid!
  - HATE mushrooms
  - LOVE the scent of vanilla
  - can't stand anyone to touch my nose
  - I save love notes from my husband
  - I have a stash of chocolate I can't find
  - need silence to write
  - shows I love: CRIMINAL MINDS, NCIS, BLACK LIST, FBI, WINCHESTERS, any cookie/chocolate/baking challenge show, X-FILES (the list continues to grow...)
  - favorite movies: MY FAIR LADY, LAKE HOUSE, ANYTHING MARVEL and most Christmas movies...

would you like a free read?

I have two books for you to choose from if you'd like to sign up for my newsletter. I send out one email a month, sharing updates, book sales, what I'm reading and even a delicious recipe I've tried that month.

Choose between Halfway to Nowhere or Stillwater Shores… just click here to join my mailing list!

Made in the USA
Middletown, DE
25 January 2023

23162997R00124